When A Boss Falls In Love 2

Tina J

Copyright 2019

Warning:

This book is strictly Urban Fiction and the story is **NOT**

REAL!

Characters will not behave the way you want them to; nor will

they react to situations the way you think they should. Some of

them may be drug addicts, kingpins, savages, thugs, rich, poor,

ho's, sluts, haters, bitter ex-girlfriends or boyfriends, people

from the past and the list can go on and on. That is what Urban

Fiction mostly consists of. If this isn't anything you foresee

yourself interested in, then do yourself a favor and don't read it

because it's only going to piss you off. ☺☺

Also, the book will not end the way you want so please be

advised that the outcome will be based solely on my own

thoughts and ideas. I hope you enjoy this book that y'all made

me write. Thanks so much to my readers, supporters, publisher

and fellow authors and authoress for the support. ☉☉

Author Tina J

More books from me:

The Thug I Chose 1, 2 & 3

A Thin Line Between Me and My Thug 1 & 2

I Got Luv For My Shawty 1 & 2

Kharis and Caleb: A Different Kind of Love 1 & 2

Loving You Is A Battle 1 & 2 & 3

Violet and The Connect 1 & 2 & 3

You Complete Me

Love Will Lead You Back

This Thing Called Love

Are We In This Together 1,2 &3

Shawty Down To Ride For a Boss 1, 2 &3

When A Boss Falls in Love 1, 2 & 3

Let Me Be The One 1 & 2

We Got That Forever Love

Aint No Savage Like The One I Got 1&2

A Queen and A Hustla 1, 2 & 3

Thirsty For A Bad Boy 1&2

Hassan and Serena: An Unforgettable Love 1&2

My Brother's Keeper 1. 2 & 3

C'Yani & Meek: A Dangerous Hood Love 1, 2 & 3

When A Savage Falls for A Good Girl 1, 2 & 3

Eva & Deray 1 & 2

Blame It On His Gangsta Luv 1 & 2

Previously...

Jesse

Today was the best day of my life since getting out of jail. My brother was probably dead and I had both of my women with me. Yup. I had Rylee and Meadow. I know you're probably wondering what I'm doing with her but its pretty funny. Rylee was the daughter of the woman I so called raped ten years ago.

You see I was sleeping with Rylee for a year before she and I came up with the plan to blackmail her mom. She and her mom never got along and hated one another with a passion. However, in order to get her mom to give her the inheritance her dad left when he died she had to get married per her mother.

We decided that she should have her money now and not have to wait for it. Anyway, I would go in and sleep with her mom but other people would call it rape. I told her if she ever told I would release the tape I had on the Internet and as a corporate lawyer she couldn't do that. We explained what she had to do in order for it not to be released and that was to change the clause for her inheritance.

A month later she did and Rylee got her money but I was obsessed with sleeping with her mom. It was like raping her was a hobby and she took it in every hole possible. Unfortunately, the bitch got smart and taped me and I got arrested and sent to jail for ten years thanks to my brother. That stupid nigga was supposed to get me off all the way but instead I spent ten years of my life behind bars. I know he's not a lawyer but his money was long and he should've done better. Rylee came to see me about two years ago and we came up with the plan to get my brother for all he had. But this crazy bitch became obsessed with Gage and fell in love.

By the time I came home he was involved with some chick named Meadow. I had no plans on fucking with her because I knew he was in love with her. However, the day I came to his house and she had that towel wrapped around her I was adamant about making her mine. The night I heard her and my brother fucking I tried my luck and opened the door. My brother had a soundproof room but the door was cracked. I peeked in and home girl was sucking the hell out of his dick.

Another night I came home and tried my luck again and the door was open. She was riding him this time and the faces she made turned me on so much I pulled my dick out and came in my hand. If Gage ever found out I did that my head would be served to my mother with no remorse.

My mom loved both of us and she was sour with him that I had to do that much time in jail too. That's why when I told her Meadow and I had a thing she was ok with making sure Gage didn't find out. The day at her house I asked her to make him leave and told her Meadow and I hadn't been able to spend time together and she made it happen. Even though my mom loved both of us she loved me more because I was the troubled child and could do no wrong in her eyes. She knew damn well I didn't have any business with my brothers' girl but she went right along with the shit.

"Damn, that was fun." Rylee said and dropped down to suck my dick. I don't know what my brother was thinking letting her go. She was the real deal when it came to sex.

"Suck all that shit out Rylee." When she was done I was ready to fuck but I didn't want her but I knew damn well I had to give Meadow some time to trust me before she gave it up. She was pregnant too. I know that it was about to have a niggas head gone.

"Tell me what happened?"

"Shit is fucked up over there."

"What you mean?"

"Something happened to Khalid's girl that she had to be put on a stretcher and taken to the hospital. I shot your brother twice in the stomach and you have his bitch. What else could we possibly need?"

"Is he dead?"

"I think so. He was talking to Bruno and flat lined."

"How did you get away?"

"After I shot him I ran in the bathroom. No one knew it was me because everyone was running in different directions. I waited five minutes and pretended I was using the bathroom. I sat back and watched it all then slipped out the back door. Look, the shit made the news." She turned the television up and we listened to her say there was a shooting and the person was still on the loose.

"What do you want to do about her?"

"After I fuck her a few times you can kill her."

"Why do you want to fuck her? You better not be in love with her?"

"Cut the shit Rylee. You're in love with my brother."

"That was before. Since you've been home it's been all about you."

"You telling me you didn't try and sleep with him tonight?"

"It was for old time's sake."

"Exactly. Get you petty ass over here so I can fuck you in the ass. I haven't done that with anyone since I left jail."

"I bet there ass didn't feel as good as mine though."

"You're right. I didn't have a pussy to play with and I damn sure wasn't touching a dick." Say what you want but if you can fuck a bitch in the ass you can do a man too and ten years will make a nigga say fuck it.

"Let's go check on this bitch." I said to Rylee when we were done. I unlocked the locks and opened the basement door.

"WHERE THE FUCK IS SHE?"

Chapter 1

Khalid

Gage called my phone while I was in the bathroom washing my hands to tell me something happened to my girl. I remember telling her to find Meadow and come back to where I was. It didn't even dawn on me that it never happened because what felt like twenty minutes was really only ten. The moment I raced out there to see what happened she was on the floor bleeding from her head with foam coming out her mouth. It doesn't take a rocket scientist to tell me something wasn't right.

I yoked Maribel up but she swore they were standing there talking and she hit the floor. Maci didn't mention any health issues to me but it also didn't mean she had none. I dropped her stupid ass and listen to her tell us Jesse was there as well. I wanted to go find him with Gage but the EMT's were putting Maci on a stretcher. I heard gunshots but I couldn't worry about anything at the moment but my girl. I turned around and Maribel was smirking as we were walking out. I swear on everything I love I will kill her if she had anything to do with what happened here.

I called Maci's parents to let them know about her. I sat there waiting for the doctors to tell me something when another ambulance pulled in with my boy Gage. There was blood all over the sheets on the stretcher and the clothes of the people that must've been working on him in the back.

"What happened to him?" I asked one of the guys who brought him. He was filling out some shit on an iPad which I later found out was information on what happened.

"Are you a relative?" He asked.

"I'm his brother."

"Your brother was shot in the stomach and flat lined twice on the way here. He lost a lot of blood and needs a transfusion. I'm not sure how bad the injuries are but by the looks of things you may want to call your parents and make them aware." He said with a gloomy look on his face.

What was supposed to be a celebration for all of us turned into a fucking nightmare? Both my girl and my brother

14

were in the hospital fighting for their life and I have no idea

why. I called Bruno's phone and he told me him and Melina

were waiting for everyone to leave and they would be up here.

Maci's mom and dad walked in and her mom had tears coming

down. Both of them gave me a hug and asked me if I heard

anything about what was going on. I told them she was still in

the back but that the doctor promised to come out the minute

he checked her. That was four hours ago. Gage's mom was

now here and we hadn't seen Melina or Bruno yet.

"The family of Maci Woods." The doctor came out

looking for us. Her parents and I stood up.

"I'm her mom, this is her dad and fiancé. Is my

daughter going to be ok?"

"We're not really sure what caused the fall that her

fiancé told us she had. However, she did suffer a lot of head

trauma and has a little swelling on the brain. Unfortunately, the

fall caused her to have a miscarriage." I heard her mom gasp.

He finished telling us that she will need a lot of rest and that

her headaches will come and go once the swelling goes down.

He shook our hand and told us once she was in a room we could visit her.

"Are you ok?" My mom asked. She came in just as the doctor was telling us what happened.

"Yea, I'm good. I was really looking forward to being a father." I felt a few tears leave my eyes and quickly wiped them away.

"I'm sorry this happened to you. God works in mysterious ways and he needed his angel back." I nodded my head at my mom. The nurse came out and informed us that Maci was in a room and we could see her but she was heavily sedated and probably would be sleep until the next day. I asked Gage's mom to call me when she heard something about him. We exchanged hugs and I went to see my girl.

****

Maci was hooked up to a few machines and sleeping peacefully. Her mom kissed her forehead and broke down in her dads' arms. I stood over the bed watching Maci and praying that she would be ok. I loved her more than I loved myself and I needed her to wake up. She wasn't in a coma or

16

anything but seeing how helpless she was and that I wasn't there to catch that fall had me hurting.

"What happened to her?" Melina came running in with tears in her eyes. I was at a loss for words so her mom told her.

"Where is Meadow and why isn't she here?" Melina wiped her eyes and I saw Bruno lean back against the wall with his head back.

"Mom, dad you need to brace yourself for what I'm about to tell you." I could see the fear in their eyes.

"Gage's brother kidnapped Meadow and no one knows where she is."

"WHAT THE FUCK YOU MEAN SHE WAS KIDNAPPED?" I don't think I ever heard him raise his voice before. His face was beet red and he was breathing heavy. Melina stood there telling us what happened and I couldn't do anything but shake my head. If Gage would've dealt with his brother from the beginning none of this would've happened.

"Daddy, it wasn't Gage's fault this time. Someone found out about the party and posted it online. After you guys left more and more people came. The party was so crowded he must've slipped in unnoticed."

"HOW THE FUCK DO YOU SLIP IN SOMEWHERE UNNOTICED?"

"Baby, calm down. I know you're upset but they're going to kick us out and I know you don't want that." Her mom said and rubbed on his chest.

"Gage, better be out looking for her."

"Honey, did you forget that someone shot him and he's in surgery?"

"What the hell happened after we left?" He asked her and she told him all that she knew. I shook my head because once Gage got up he was going to declare war on any and every one that had something to do with Meadow's disappearance; including his mother.

A few hours later everyone left and I stayed to make sure my baby saw me when she opened her eyes. That medicine must've been some strong shit because she did not get up. I asked the nurses for a blanket. I pulled that chair out and got comfortable. This was going to be a long night.

Chapter 2

Maribel

You damn right I'm happy something happened to that bitch. I'm not about to sit around and let her be happy with my man. Khalid had money, he was smart and his sex game put a bitch to sleep after the first round. Shit, she is living my happily ever after and I'm going to do everything in my power to make sure she doesn't get it. I know I told Khalid I wanted him to be happy but it had to be with me. Yea, I cheated on him but that's because he was neglecting me. He was a great man but he spent so much time at work; that my needs were unattended. I should've and could've spoken to him about it but hell if he wasn't sleeping with me then he had to know someone else was going to handle that.

I only cheated on him with one guy; but multiple times. My fuck up was not making his dumb ass strap up and ended up pregnant. I truly believed it was Khalid's because I was three months when I found out. I had stop taking my birth control a few months prior to the last time he and I had sex. I loved the hell out of Khalid and I wanted us to have a family.

19

Unfortunately, we hadn't had sex once I stopped taking them but I assumed me getting pregnant was an accident by him. You know they say it can still happen on the pill so I thought that's what happened.

There was a big raid at his house and I just knew the Feds were going to find something and keep him for years. However, his money went a long way and he was home sooner than later. The day he came by the dude I was messing with had just left. I was getting out the shower and Khalid was sitting on my bed shaking his head.

"You know it's over right?" He said burning a hole in my face.

"What are you talking about and how did you get out?" I asked standing there in the same spot. He stood up and walked towards me.

"Maribel, I have never cheated on you or even entertained another woman while we were together. The minute I get locked up you hop in the bed with another man." I went to speak but he stopped me.

"There's no need to explain because I saw it with my

own eyes."

"Khalid, I've been lonely and you were too busy for me."

"Fuck that. You were my woman. If you felt neglected at any time you could've come to where I was and got some dick. Don't try and justify what you did. I gave you everything your heart desired. There was nothing I wouldn't have done for you but because I was busy with work and school you cheat. You had the key to my house and if you needed me you should've told me. But it's all-good. I hope he makes you happy." *He went to turn around and I jumped in front of him dropping my towel. He smirked and bent down to pick it up for me.*

"You may have got that but those hickeys on your neck proves that I'm making the right choice in leaving you alone." *He slammed the door and walked out. I threw my robe on and went running off him but he was pulling off before I opened the screen door. I fell to my knees and cried all night. Weeks and months went by and I tried constantly to get him to take me back. I don't know how many times I went to his house or club*

and stripped naked and he still wasn't beat for me.

When I walked in the party and saw how happy those two were my blood was boiling. But being the fake bitch that I am I played it off well. I saw Rylee step in and I knew off the back Khalid was going to jump up to go warn Gage. But when Jesse walked in that was a shocker. I hadn't seen him in years and from what Rylee told me he was trying real hard to get at Meadow. I'm sure everyone is well aware that Jesse was bitter that Gage couldn't get him off for the burglary charge but truth be told his ass should still be in jail. I saw Jesse take the steps two at a time and I knew all hell was about to break loose.

"Why does that name Jesse sound familiar?" I heard Maci say. I was reaching in my purse as I told her it was Gage's brother. The look of shock on her face was evident and it gave me time to stab her ass in the neck with the needle I had full of cyanide. I was sick of this bitch and this as the best way to get her. There would be no trace of it in her system and they had to be looking at for it on order to find it. Her body started shaking and in seconds she hit the floor. Thank goodness no one was in the same room. When I saw the blood start leaking out I had to put on my acting roll and scream out for someone to get her man; well my man. Damn that sounds good rolling off my tongue again.

He snatched me up and tried to kill me until Gage got him to loosen his grip. I watched him cradle her while he waited for the EMT's. I saw her body convulse and the foam start dripping out. She was taking too long to die. The medical team came in and saw her and jabbed some shit in her leg. It seemed to stop her from dying and a bitch was pissed. They threw her on the stretcher and rushed her out with Khalid right behind. I snatched my shit up and left the house.

Chapter 3

Meadow

After I heard what happened on my street and that crazy asshole left I started looking for anything to get out. There was nothing down here but tools and a few boxes of videotapes. It was some other crap in there but I didn't find what I needed. The television was still on and I heard the woman from the news channel come back on. I listened to her say one person was shot and another passed out but still had no leads on who the shooter was. I used the bathroom that was down here and had to shake my pussy dry because there was no tissue. I heard the front door open and close and sat at the top of the stairs to listen to dumb and dumber discuss what happen. I couldn't believe not only were they working and sleeping together but also that bitch shot my man.

"Let's go see what the fuck the bitch is down there doing." I heard Jesse say and footsteps coming towards the door. I ran and hid under the steps that had a hidden door. They both walked down talking shit about how he was going to fuck me and then she could kill me. I was in awe at how much hate they had towards me but for Jesse to have hated his brother like that was worse. Gage did what he could to help him but he was holding a grudge.

"Where the fuck is she?" I heard Jesse yell out and heard them running around the basement. It was a decent size but not enough to have them running back and forth like idiots. I heard someone by the door I was in and peeked out of it. It was the Rylee bitch. I yanked her by the back of her hair and started raining blows to her face over and over. I could feel someone lifting me in the air.

"Get the fuck off of her." He yelled and tossed me across the room. I was able to catch myself from falling and went to run up the steps. He grabbed me by my hair and pulled me back down the three steps I had climbed. The hits he gave me didn't do anything but make me fight back harder. He and I were going blow for blow. My left eye was closing but I refused to give up. He kicked me in my chest so hard I went flying back into the wall. The wind was knocked out of my body and I fell to the floor; however I didn't pass out. I watched him rush over to her and that's when I remembered what I had. I lifted myself up with all the strength I had left. His back was turned. I ran towards him and stabbed his ass in the back over and over with the screwdriver. He screamed out and fell backwards.

"I'm going to kill you bitch." He said in between breaths.

"Not if you're dead." I kicked him a few times then bent down to get his cell phone.

"What's the password?" I asked him when I noticed it was locked.

"Fuck you bitch." I took my hand and pressed the screwdriver down in his stomach.

"Ahhh." He screamed out and I asked him again. This nigga refused to give it to me. I stabbed him a few more times then went over and did the same thing to Rylee.

"That's for shooting my man. You stupid bitch." She screamed louder and louder. *Shit, I just killed them. I'm going to jail. Think, think Meadow. What would Gage tell you to do if you were ever in a situation like this? Cover your tracks.* And that's just what I did. I looked under the kitchen sink and found some yellow cleaning gloves and put them on.

"FUCK ME." I doubled over and grabbed the table as I felt excruciated pain in my stomach. I was sure to be having a miscarriage but I couldn't focus on that or any other pain I was having. My one eye was completely shut but I had to keep going. I started wiping down anything I touched in the basement and upstairs. I grabbed the car keys off the table and put them in my pocket.

I went to the kitchen and found a lighter. I set some paper towels on fire and let the shit sit on the couch. The flame caught on pretty fast. I ran out to the car with a throw blanket I found on the couch and sat it in the driver's seat. I had liquids coming down my leg but I wanted to make sure I had no DNA in this vehicle. I drove back to my house and no one was there. Caution tape was up and there was a notice on the door telling me to contact the detective who left his card. I went inside and grabbed the house phone.

"Melina."

"Meadow. Is that you?" I could hear her screaming in the phone.

"Yes sis. I need you." Now that I was sitting and my adrenaline wasn't pumping as much all the pain-starting kicking in.

"Where are you? I'm coming for you."

"I'm back at the house. Please hurry. I think I'm dying."

"Meadow. Hold on." That was the last thing I heard before I blacked out.

****

"Are you ok Meadow?" I heard my dad's voice as I opened my eyes.

"Where am I?" I tried lifting myself up but the pain was so bad I laid back down.

The machines started going off and the nurses came running in to check. The doctor walked in not too long after giving me the bad news. I expected it but I wasn't as sad as I thought I would be because I knew it. There was no way I took that beating and my baby made it. I wiped my eyes and nodded my head as he told me I had a few bruised ribs. My eye was red and he told me I would have to see a specialist to make sure there was no damage.

"How long have I been here?" I asked the doctor and looked over at my dad who seemed to have a lot on his mind.

"You've been here for three days ma'am."

"Three days. It doesn't feel like that. Where is Gage?" Has he come to see me yet?" The doctor looked at me funny and my dad told him he would explain everything to me.

"Baby, Gage is still in a coma. He lost so much blood from the shooting that he his body went into shock and then a coma. The doctors said his lung collapsed and he had."

"No, no, no. Daddy take me to him please." I screamed out and tossed the covers back. I didn't care that the machines were going haywire. I needed to see him.

"Calm down Meadow."

"Daddy, if he hears my voice he will wake up. Please take me to him." I was hysterical crying. The nurse came in and brought me a wheelchair. I looked at her strangely and she said that someone by the name of Bruno told her the minute I asked to see him she was to take me. She also told me he paid her very well and that she had to give him what he paid for. She hooked the IV bag on the pole that was on the chair and helped me in. My dad just shook his head and walked behind us. The elevator door opened up and she wheeled me to the nurse's station. The minute she wheeled me in his room I broke down crying. He had a breathing machine on him and tubes going in his nose and mouth. I tried to stand and almost fell but my father caught me and put me back in the chair. I asked them both to excuse me for a few minutes while I spoke to him.

"Gage baby. It's me your fiancé. I know you're resting right now but I need you to wake up." I rubbed his hand and kissed it. I thought about telling him we lost the baby but I decided to wait. I've heard so many times that when you tell a person bad news while they're in a coma it causes more stress because they can't move. I don't want that for him.

"I love you so much baby. Please wake up." I laid my head down on the bed and cried until I couldn't cry anymore. I put my head up to wipe my eyes and my baby was staring down at me with a few tears of his own.

"Oh my God. NURSE." I screamed out trying to get someone's attention.

"What's wrong Meadow?" My dad beat the nurse inside. I pointed to Gage who was trying to remove the tube out his throat and nose. He ended up getting it out and there was green gook on the wall from it. The shit was quite disgusting.

"Meadow are you ok?" He asked just above a whisper. The nurse brought him some water. He drank some and looked back at me.

"I am now." He smiled and my dad helped me up to get in bed with him.

"I'm going to check on Maci and I'll be back."

"Maci? What happened to Maci?" My father didn't say anything and stood there silent.

"Dad, what happened to my sister?"

"Meadow, just know that whoever did this to you and your sister are dead when I find out who they are." He kissed my forehead and walked out the door. I have never heard my father speak like that in my life.

31

"Daddy." I tried to get up and follow him but Gage pulled me back and told me to relax and that I could see her later.

Chapter 4

Gage

I thought I was going to die once I started feeling the pain of being shot. The burning sensation felt like my insides were on fire and nothing would stop it. The only thing that stayed on my mind was if my girl and unborn baby were ok. I found out she was pregnant right before I fell down the steps. The doctor said I died two times and they brought me back. His must've wanted me to live and handle my brother and that's what I planned on doing. I was lying in that coma and listened to everyone talk to me but Meadow made me think they never found her until I heard her voice. The more I listened to her talk and cry it made me fight harder to open my eyes. She was sitting in a wheelchair with a hospital gown on.

"Baby, I know you're worried about your sister but you have to get better too." She laid her head on my shoulder and started crying again.

"Baby what's wrong?" I asked.

"I lost the baby." She said and I tensed up. The

machines went off and the nurses came running in. I tried to sit up and snatch the wire off but Bruno walked in and stopped me.

"What the fuck Gage? You need to relax." I heard him say but I wasn't trying to hear it.

"Gage please stop." I heard Meadow crying. I was so mad that it took them sedating me to calm me. A few hours later I woke up again and Bruno and Khalid were in the room talking amongst themselves. I laid there listening to them.

"Where's Meadow?"

"She went back to her room to get discharged. The doctor said she was good to go. She told us to tell you she was going home and she would be back up later."

"I don't want her at the house alone."

"Her pops is going with her. Yo, her dad flipped the fuck out when he found out what happened. I didn't even know Jewish people cursed." Khalid said making us all laugh. I had to contain mine due to all the pain I was feeling. Bruno told me everything that happened with my brother and Rylee.

"Did you get rid of everything? Did you burn the car?"

"Come on man. You don't even have to ask." Khalid

said.

"I know man. I can't imagine her sitting in a jail over some shit I should've handled a long time ago. I know y'all blame me for this and you have every right too. I was just trying to give him the benefit of the doubt. I'm still trying to wrap my mind around the fact that my own brother could and would do something like this to me." I saw them both shake their heads. Their silence let me know they felt the same way. These were my boys, more or less my brothers and I should've listened to them. All the years we've known one another we have never fought over anything like we have over Jesse.

"All we can do now is focus on getting that nigga." Bruno said standing up looking out the window.

"Hold up. I thought you said the house burned up." I said looking at both of them.

"It did. However, someone saw the fire before it got bad and called the fire department. They were able to get it out before it reached the basement. Those two were down there barely hanging on. The cops moved them to an undisclosed location." Khalid said and I have them the side eye

"Exactly. You know we have the place covered." Bruno said. There's nothing we couldn't find out with the type of bosses we were. We stayed there talking for a while and I found out Maci lost her baby too and was still sleeping. Meadow came back up to the hospital and gave me a sponge bath in bed. She refused to allow any of the nurses to touch me. Her excuse was no other woman needed to see what was hers. I just laughed. Housekeeping came in and changed my bedding as well.

"I'm sorry baby." I whispered and ran my hand down her face. Her eye was still bruised and her side was in pain.

"It's ok Gage. God wasn't ready for us to have another one until we got all the negativity out of our lives. We both know his time is coming." She leaned in and pecked my lips before getting in bed beside me. I loved the hell out of this woman and I was going to do everything I could to make sure she stayed safe.

****

It had been five weeks since the shooting and a nigga was happy as home he got the green light to go home. Khalid

36

was up here at the crack of dawn to get me. Meadow wasn't feeling that at all because she wanted to pick me up. I took a shower and threw on the gray Jordan sweat suit she sent up for me with my gray and white Jordan's. The doctor gave me the discharge papers and we were out. I had Khalid take me to the store to pick up a few things before I got home. Yes, I went back to the same house everything happened in. I tried to get Meadow to move but she said no and that this was her dream house and no one was running her out.

I opened the door and it looked as if it was brand new with furniture. Bruno told me he had it professionally cleaned and had some new rugs put in the living room from where Maci fell and started bleeding. Meadow had the people come and install a top of the line security system that had cameras everywhere in and outside of the house. I didn't think we needed them when we brought the house because it was in a secluded area and no one knew where we lived but I was wrong. I smelled some food coming from the kitchen and it was my girl standing there naked in just an apron and heels. She looked sexy as fuck and my dick stood straight up. I was glad Khalid dropped me off and bounced.

"You like what you see?" She asked me without turning around. I lifted my shirt over my head and kicked my sneakers off.

"Hell yea I do." I kissed the back of her neck and watched her turn the food off. She turned around and put her arms around my neck and hopped in my arms.

"It's all your baby. Do what you want to me?" Our tongues found the inside on each other's mouth and performed a show of its own. I backed up and had her body against the wall.

"Put me down Gage." I was surprised but did what she said. I felt my sweats and boxers come down. Her mouth was covering my dick in no time. Now I was against the wall receiving the best head in the world from my woman. I stared at her as she allowed me to make love to her face. In and out my dick went and each time she took in more and more of it. I felt the nut brewing and came so hard I had to catch myself from falling.

"Mmmmm baby. Now that, that's out of the way you

can fuck me without coming quick." I chuckled and helped her stand up.

"Let me taste you."

"I thought you would say that." She dropped the apron, hopped up on the counter and spread her legs wide open for me. My mouth watered as I came face to face with what I had been craving for in the hospital. The second my tongue touched her clit she came instantly.

"Damn, it's been a long time Gage. Now eat this pussy like you missed it." That shit turned me on so much I went crazy eating her out. Her hips were fucking my face as I made her cum over and over. I slid her down on my dick and dug so deep she tried to jump off.

"Nah Meadow. This is what you wanted. Take all this dick." I carried her over to the couch with me still inside her and dug deeper and deeper.

"Shit Gage. You're rearranging my insides."

"Good, turn over." Once she did that I smacked her ass and watched it jiggle.

"Oh God Gage, here I cum again baby. Sssss." She

moaned out and I saw her wet my dick up. I made love to her and fucked her for the next few hours until we both came a few more times.

"I love you Meadow." I moved the hair out her face as we laid there on the living room floor naked.

"I love you too Gage." She kissed my lips and stood up. I followed behind her as she walked upstairs and we both took a shower. I came out the bathroom and she had candles lit and both of our plates were on a tray sitting on the bed.

"What's this?"

"I wanted to have dinner in bed." She came and sat next to me. She and I ate dinner together. Afterwards I took our trays downstairs and straightened up the kitchen since she cooked. I turned everything off, went back upstairs and found her knocked out. I turned the television on and wasn't too far behind her.

Chaapter 5

Khalid

It's been over two months and Maci was still sleeping like she was in a coma; only she wasn't. The nurse told me she woke up a few times but complained about a headache so she gave her pain medication for it. Something in my gut was telling me everything about what I was hearing was suspect. I called Melina up and asked her could she come sit at the hospital with her. I had been staying up there every night but during the day I would run a few errands and have her mom or dad checking in on her. The way I was feeling now had me not wanting her to be alone. I pulled up at Gage's house and parked.

"Hey you." Meadow said answering the door holding Melina's daughter Morgan. She reached out for me and I took her from her aunt who was talking shit because of it. Bruno's daughter was a few months old and she was already spoiled as hell by all of us. I sat on the couch waiting for Gage to come down. I imagined what my child would've looked like if Maci didn't have a miscarriage.

"What's up bro?"

"Nothing. I wanted to ask you something." Meadow was sitting on the other couch watching television. He nodded his head at her I guess to see if she could stay. I told him it was fine.

"Maci, has been sleep for a long time and she's not in a coma. I feel like something ain't right." I went on to tell them how her nurse said she woke up but would complain each time about the pain and give her medicine. I also told them how I had a feeling that Maribel knows more than what she was saying. Of course Meadow flipped the hell out and wanted to go out and find her. She was cursing so loud she scared Morgan and caused her to cry.

"Auntie sorry Morgan. Let's go get some bananas." She took her from me and went in the kitchen.

"If you feel like shit is suspect call up Hailey and have her go take a look at her." Hailey was a chick we went to school with that Gage used to mess with that became a doctor. She was married with kids but she always told us if we needed her to call and that's just what I did. Because she lived in Maryland and couldn't get here until Thursday and today was

Monday she told me to have her discharged to my home under her care. She gave me all the information I needed to do that and Maci was home before the night was out. I hired the same nurse to come to my house and tend to her during the daytime hours.

"Khalid, where are you?" I heard Melina yelling through my house. We all had keys to one another's house and the girls made sure they did the same. I closed the door to the room Maci was staying in and walked down the steps to where she was. I saw her and the nurse having a stare down but I didn't know why. I told the nurse she could leave for the evening and would see her tomorrow.

"What's up Melina?" I asked grabbing a water out the fridge. I turned around and her arms were across her chest and she had an evil look on her face.

"I don't like that bitch."

"What bitch?" I asked laughing at her. Out of all the sisters Melina was the most violent of the three.

"Khalid, I know Maci is your fiancé but at the end of the day she is my sister. I don't know what's going on but

43

something is fishy with that nurse. Not only that why hasn't she woke up yet? She isn't in a coma and the doctors can't seem to figure it out either." I nodded my head letting her know I understood because I felt the same way.

"The doctor comes in tomorrow to check on her so if anything is going on she will be able to tell."

"I don't want that nurse around Maci anymore."

"She's done for the night anyway. I will send her a text telling her she isn't needed for tomorrow. Is that ok?"

"For now it is." She went upstairs and sat with her sister for a while. After she left I hopped in the shower and laid in bed with her. She looked so perfect lying there and all I could do was stare. The IV was still in her arm to dispense medication. I watched television until I went to sleep.

The next day I got up early to make sure I was dressed when Hailey came. I had Meadow come by to wash Maci up. The doorbell rung and when I opened it I heard Meadow start yelling. Both Hailey and I went running up the stairs and into the room Maci was in.

"What's up Meadow?" She pointed to Maci's stomach and she had black and blue marks on it. She rolled her over and there were more up and down her back. I didn't know what the hell was going on and why she was marked up like that but you could believe I was getting to the bottom of it. Hailey asked the both of us to remove ourselves from the room while she examined her. I noticed the two women give each other a once over. I'm not sure if Gage informed Meadow that this was his ex but I damn sure didn't want any drama right now.

"Khalid, where do you think those marks came from?" She paced the floor as we waited for the doctor to come out.

"I have no idea Meadow but I'm telling you now the person is dead when I find out." I poured myself a shot of patron to calm my nerves. I was ready to fuck some shit up and I think she knew. I heard her on the phone with Melina telling her to have the guys come by but I was fine.

"Khalid, I took some blood from her and did an exam. As of right now there's no indication of why she's still asleep after all this time. I want you to tell the nurse that you have come by to call me the second Maci wakes up. If she is in pain

45

I want to ask her what they are and figure out what's causing it. There could be something else wrong with her but we won't know that until she tells us." She left me her hotel information and said she was staying for a few days. She was putting a rush on her blood work to see if anything was going on.

"Thanks Hailey. I appreciate you dropping everything and coming here to check on her." I hugged her and walked her to the door.

"How has he been?" She tried to ask me quietly but Meadow heard her at the same time he walked in the door. The two of them stood there staring at each other.

"WHAT THE FUCK GAGE?" Meadow yelled and stormed out the house. This right here was going to be a problem. I heard a car screech and I knew she was pissed and I think Gage did too.

"I'll be back Khalid." He raced out the door and hopped in his car. Bruno stepped in shaking his head.

"What was that about?" Hailey asked when I walked her to the car.

"That was his fiancé."

"Oh. I didn't know."

"I know but the way you both stood there staring at each other would make me mad too."

"I was just shocked to see him after all these years."

"I'm sure the feeling was mutual but knowing his girl the way I do she felt disrespected. I'm sure you would feel the same way." I walked back in the house and shut the door. Hailey is cool don't get me wrong but calling her may not have been the right thing to do. She was obsessed over Gage so bad that he had to get a restraining order on her ass.

"You know that's going to be a problem right?" Bruno said walking in the room with a glass of Henney in his hand.

"I know but I needed someone I could trust to check my girl out."

"I get it man. Just make sure you send her ass straight the fuck back home after you find out." I nodded my head and had a drink with him.

****

Two days went by and I didn't hear from Hailey and told the nurse her services were no longer needed. I was getting out the shower when I swore I saw Maci moving. I ran over to the bed not caring that my towel fell.

"Khalid." I heard her whisper and felt some tears leaving my eyes. I don't know if I was shedding them because she was awake or the fact that I was who she called out for. I kissed her lips and her eyes popped open and she smiled. She tried to sit up and put her hand on her head.

"Thank you for coming back to me." I said and she ran her hand down my face.

"I couldn't leave you baby."

"How are you feeling? Is your head ok?" I asked as I kissed her face over and over. I missed the hell out of my girl.

"I feel fine baby. How long was I asleep?" When I told her she covered her mouth? She asked where everyone was and wanted me to put her in the shower before I called and told them she was awake. She tried to stand but her legs were weak I guess from not being in use. I carried her in the bathroom and put her hands on the rail so she could hold herself up while I washed her. I dressed her and took her downstairs as we waited for everyone to show up.

"Khalid, I don't understand why I was asleep so long. I woke up a few times but each time I told the nurse to contact you she kept telling me she was giving me something for the pain. The crazy part is I didn't tell her I was hurting. Khalid I called for you every time. Where were you?" The shit she said tugged at my heart.

"Maci I was there all day every day and I stayed the night. I left after the first two days to handle business but I made sure someone was there checking on you. Maci, I'm sorry that this happened to you. I'm going up to the hospital tomorrow and you already know what's going to happen to the nurse." She shook her head and pulled my face to hers.

"Mmmmm, I missed you." I felt my man rising off that kiss and pulled myself away from her.

"What's wrong? You don't want me anymore?" I could see the hurt in her face and her eyes got glossy.

"Never that baby. I will always want you. It's just that your family will be here in a minute and you just woke up. I'm giving you time to get back into the swing of things."

"Khalid, I was only sleeping and that kiss has my pussy dripping and calling out for you. Please make love to me." She slid her pants off and climbed on top of me and pulled my man out with no hesitation.

"Maci, let's do this later." Her mouth covered mine as she slid down and sat there. "Shit baby. You don't know how much I missed you." She put her face in my neck and sucked and licked on it. I lifted her body up and guided it up and down. Her walls were squeezing the hell out of me.

"Khalid, I'm about to cum." She moaned in my ear.

"Me too baby." It's been so long that neither of us could hold out. I pumped faster under her as she tried to bounce hard on me. I know she needed to get used to it again.

"Shit Maci. This pussy is the best. Ahhh." She and I both came at the same time. I heard car doors closing as we sat there kissing. My dick was rising again but we had to stop. I lifted her up and took us in the bathroom to clean up. When we walked out I saw Melina smirking with Bruno coming in behind her looking like he wanted to ask what was going on but didn't. Melina hugged Maci so tight she had to yell at her to make her stop. Meadow and her parents came in and it was like the crying game between the women.

"Where's Gage?" Maci asked Meadow.

"Who the fuck knows and I hope he stays away?" I saw my girl look at me and I shrugged my shoulders. Gage told me Meadow was still tripping off that day Hailey came by. Oh well that was a problem I wasn't involving myself in unless he asked. I had my girl by my side and I wasn't doing anything to lose her.

Chapter 6

Maci

The day all that shit happened at my sisters' house I woke up a few days later looking for Khalid and my family.

Some nurse came in and asked me if I had any pain and I told her no but she insisted I did and said she was giving me pain medicine to help. This happened every time I woke up and I didn't understand why. When I woke up this last time I was ecstatic that my fiancé was there and I wouldn't be put back to sleep. He washed me up and gave me a quickie on the couch before my family came but after they left he made love to me until I couldn't take anymore. This man was so good to me that I wanted to do something nice for him.

A few days went by and he told me he was going to be at the office but if I needed anything to call him. I know my baby was busy and worried about me so I decided to surprise him. I got to the club and it was a few people there that were happy to see me. I got along with all his employees and they respected me in return. I saw Gage talking to some chick in his office and he looked angry but I kept going. I sent my sister a text to tell her what was going on but she said fuck him. My next stop was her job when I left to find out what was really going on with them.

I opened Khalid's office and he had his back turned as he talked on the phone. I walked over and placed soft kisses on his neck and slid my hand down his shirt to rub on his chest. He turned around and kissed my lips and told me to hold on one second. I kneeled down in front of him and unbuckled his jeans. He tried to stop me but I wasn't having that and smacked his hand away. I pulled his man out and kissed the tip before running my tongue up and down his shaft.

"Sssss." He said. The caller must've asked if he was ok and he told them yes. I relaxed my jaw muscles and went all the way down.

"Ohhhh shittttttttt." He moaned out on the phone.

"Yo, I have to call you back." He told the caller and hung the phone up. I could hear him struggling to put it on the receiver as I bobbed up and down just the way he liked it. I licked under his balls and took each one in my mouth separately. He was running his hands through my hair as I took him to ecstasy.

"Suck it all baby." I removed all his sperm and swallowed it like a drink. He snatched me up and sat me on his lap.

"What was that for?" He lifted my shirt and sucked gently on each of my breast.

"Just because I love you."

"I love you too." He fucked me straight to sleep in his office. I'm not kidding. After we finished I fell asleep on the couch in there and stayed until he woke me up for us to leave. We made our way through the now crowded club and went to our cars. We got home and found Meadow sitting in the living room watching television and eating popcorn like this was her place. She had bags under eyes like she had been crying. Khalid kissed me and went upstairs to give us privacy.

"What's up sis? Why you over here looking like a lost puppy?"

"Gage, is cheating on me and I don't want to look in his face right now." I covered my mouth and sat next to her. She put her head on my shoulders and cried harder. I asked why she assumed he was cheating and the things she told me would make me suspect but not positive. I told her to ask him but she said all men cheat and he would probably lie anyway.

"Meadow, you're my sister and you know there's no issue with you staying here but don't you think you should hear him out first?"

"I don't want to look at his lying ass right now." I heard the door slam and it was Gage looking pissed off. She rolled her eyes and went to get up.

"What the fuck Meadow? It's been almost a week and your ass ain't been home. I tried to give you your space to sort through whatever is wrong with you but you're bringing your ass home tonight." I saw Khalid coming down the steps with a concerned look on his face.

"Fuck you Gage. Take your ass back to that fake ass doctor bitch that you've been spending time with." I saw the shocked look on his face.

"Yea nigga. You thought you were the only one that can find information out. Just remember everyone knows we're together and when they saw another chick at the restaurant with you they thought maybe you were in a business meeting

55

until they saw you doing this." She showed him her phone and it was him engaged in a kiss with another woman.

"Let me explain that Meadow."

"Nah, there's no need for explanation. It's all right here. I knew something was going to happen between the two of you when I saw how you looked at each other the first day she came by."

"Meadow, there's nothing going on with her."

"Pictures are worth a thousand words Gage. I know you see this photo just like I do." Meadow started crying harder and he tried to comfort her but she ran in the bathroom and locked the door. The doorbell rang and Khalid went to answer it. Some woman walked in and she was very pretty. She looked to be about five foot six with a caramel complexion. Her eyes were hazel and you could tell she had a nice body by the way her clothes clung to her. I felt some kind of way and stood in front of my man.

"Baby, she doesn't have shit on you on your worse day." He whispered in my ear and kissed my neck. That boosted my confidence but she was still a bit intimidating.

"Maci, it's good to see that you're awake." I glanced up at Khalid and he explained who she was.

"Thank you. How can we help you?"

"Well I came by to tell you that your blood work came back normal but one of them came back with small levels of cyanide in it."

"WHAT THE FUCK YOU MEAN CYANIDE WAS IN HER BLOOD?" Khalid yelled out scaring both of us. She went on to tell us that when the blood work came back it was normal but the levels in one of them was extremely abnormal so they continued testing it for all sorts of things and that's what the results were. She told us to find the nurse that took care of me and question her. The only thing was he went to the hospital the day after I woke up and they said she just up and quit with no reason and they haven't seen her since. The name she gave my man wasn't even her real name, which was making it harder for him to find her. He hired a private detective and was waiting on him to get back to us.

"Hello Gage." She said looking past us and licking her lips. Meadow must've caught that shit because in five seconds flat she was beating the hell out of the doctor. It took Gage a few minutes to get her off but my sister left her face leaking.

"Keep your woman under control Gage. The next time I will press charges on her." Gage had her up against the wall by her shirt yelling in her face.

"I wish the fuck you would. Stay the fuck away from me and my girl and if you even think about getting the law involved I will kill all three of those kids." I saw the fear on her face but had no remorse. She didn't say shit and walked out the door. Meadow went up into the guest room and locked the door.

"Fuck this shit man. These women are driving me fucking crazy." He said and slammed the door. I felt bad for Gage because he had Rylee missing in action, this doctor bitch came back from the dead starting shit and my sister wasn't talking to him. I didn't say anything and watched my man lock the house up and put the alarm on.

"I knew that bitch was going to be a problem." Khalid said and carried me up to the room.

"What you mean baby?" I asked him getting undressed to take a shower. He told me who she was and how she did nothing but cause problems in Gage's life. I don't know what type of women Gage dealt with but the one thing that was clear was they were all crazy over him but all he wanted was my sister. He better get that shit together because no one was going to come for her.

Chapter 7

Gage

I know y'all think a nigga ain't shit but before you go

judging let me explain. The day Hailey came to help Maci that

was the first time I saw her in over four years. Hailey and I

used to mess around but I never made her my girl; yet we were

exclusive to one another. I didn't sleep with anyone while I

messed with her. She was a few years older than me and had

just started medical school. Anyway, we messed around for a

few months before she told me that she was in love with me. I

told her the feelings were not the same and maybe we should

take a break. The bitch lost it and started threatening to stand in

front of a train to kill herself. I told her to go ahead and I may

attend her funeral.

Unfortunately, she didn't do it and I had to endure a lot

of bullshit with her. I started seeing another woman and Hailey

found out, followed her to work and ran her over with her car.

Another chick was with me at a restaurant and Hailey tried

fighting her in the bathroom. How she found out I was there

was beyond me. The last straw was when I tried to start my car

and there was sugar in my gas tank with a note on my

windshield that said I wouldn't be driving to see any bitch

today. It may sound like a bitch move but getting a restraining order was the best thing I could do without killing her.

Now I did tell my boy to call her but I didn't expect to be there at any time she was because I knew she would turn into that crazy chick again. The day I was at the restaurant I was meeting up with a wedding planner to marry Meadow. She's been through two miscarriages and the crap with my brother and all I wanted to do was alleviate any stress from her and give her the perfect wedding. The woman walked outside to use the phone and Hailey came up and started talking about wanting a chance to taste the dick one more time. I told that crazy bitch to get the fuck out of there. She leaned over while I was looking down on my phone and kissed me; catching me off guard. I pushed her ass so hard she hit the floor. I tried to explain that to Meadow but she wasn't trying to hear any of it. I left the house and went to bar to have a few drinks and the bitch walked in a few minutes later. I swear she was stalking me worse than Rylee.

"What the fuck you want Hailey?" She sat next to me with a smirk on her face. I noticed the cut under her eye and the busted lip she tried to hide under lipstick.

"Why are you treating me this way?"

"Are you serious?" She looked at me. I sipped my drink and went to the bathroom. I was washing my hands when she came in and locked the door. I didn't even know local bars had locks on them.

"Get the fuck out of my way." I moved past her and she grabbed my pants down. This was one of those days that I wish I had a belt on. I bent down to pull them back up and she had my boxers down and my dick in her mouth. I'm not going to lie and say I tried to stop her because I didn't. I raped her mouth like it was nothing. I heard her gagging and didn't give a fuck. If this is what she wanted I was going to give it to her. I let my nut go all over her face. She opened her legs and started playing with her pussy and instead of walking away I rammed my shit inside her. I forgot how good her pussy was and ended up fucking her in different positions. I pulled out when I felt myself getting ready to cum. I jerked myself off and came in my hand. I refused to allow anything to go in her; not even my pre cum.

"Damn that dick is as good as I remember." She said and hearing her voice brought me back to reality of what I just did. Meadow was all that I needed in a woman and I wasn't cheating on her. That's why it was going to be hard as hell telling her that I slipped up and did it. But I'm a man and I have to face the consequences because I should've known better. I heard banging on the door and I opened it to find Meadow standing on the other side smiling.

"Hey baby. I know I'm supposed to be mad at you but I just found out something and I wanted you to know first. I figured you were in here since I didn't see you. She was grinning from ear to ear; that is until she saw who was in there with me. I noticed her backing up and the tears flew down her face quickly.

"Meadow, I'm sorry. It just happened."

"Nigga, nothing just happens and why was she in here with you anyway."

"That nigga miss this pussy and I must say my pussy missed him." I heard Hailey say cracking up behind me. Meadow didn't say anything and nodded her head. I followed her out the club and to her car to talk to her.

"Meadow."

"Don't Gage. I don't want to hear it."

"Meadow, I'm sorry. She came in the bathroom while I was using it. Next thing I know she locked the door. I pushed past her but she got my pants and boxers down and went to sucking my dick." I could see her face get tight but I may as well be honest with her.

"Then what, you couldn't leave?"

"She started playing with herself and I fell victim to her and fucked her. I messed up Meadow and if you never want to see me again I understand. I'm a grown ass man and I'm not going to sit here and make a ton of excuses when at the end of the day I could've stopped it if I really wanted to."

"You're saying you wanted to fuck her."

"I'm not saying that at all. What I'm saying is I was drinking, she caught me with my pants down; literally and

64

once she sucked my dick I already fucked up so I went ahead and gave her what she wanted."

"Oh ok. The way I see it is you both wanted it. Gage, if you didn't want to you would've left her standing there without sliding your dick in her mouth or pussy. I'm glad you're not making excuses and stepping up to tell me the truth. I can respect that but what I can't respect is the way you disrespected our relationship. What we had was supposed to be solid? I have been through so much just to be with you and this is what I get in return." I felt like shit because I know she was talking about my brother and losing the babies.

"Are you stopping by my hotel after you've handled whatever this is?" Hailey said pointing back to me and Meadow.

"Yo, get the fuck out of here. What goes on between me and my girl is none of your business. Take your ass back to wherever you came from." I still called her my girl because I wasn't about to let her think she messed anything up. I saw her get in her car and pull off mad as hell.

"That is my house and I expect you to have your shit out of there by tomorrow night. I will be staying at my parent's tonight and I don't plan on saying anything to anyone right now. I would appreciate if you did the same."

"I know I messed up but can I get another chance?" She laughed in my face and left. I deserved that but what she didn't realize was she and I were forever and there was no way in hell I was letting her go. I was going to give her some space but you can believe the only way she was getting rid of me was death and I meant that shit.

****

A few months went by since Meadow caught me in the bathroom with that crazy ass doctor. Khalid told me all she did was go to work, talk to her sisters on the phone and go home. A nigga was missing her like crazy. I sent her cards; gifts and other things but they were all returned. I know she could care less how much money I had and these gifts were me trying to get back with her but she wasn't having it. I tried stopping by but she had a metal gate put up that you needed a code to get in with. The shit was high as hell and no one in their right mind would be able to climb it. I guess with me not being there this made her feel safer.

"Hello." I answered my phone with a big ass grin on my face when I saw it was her.

"Can you meet me at the Olive Garden in twenty minutes?" She asked and I told her yes. I was sitting at the office going over paperwork so I wasn't busy anyway. I saw her car and parked next to it. I walked in and told the host who I was looking for and she led me over to Meadow. She looked beautiful as she sat there gazing out the window and twirling her straw in her drink.

"Hey." I sat down and had the waitress get me a soda.

"Hi." She was dry with it. I could tell she didn't want to be here but she called me. We didn't say much to one another. I stared at her and something about her changed but I couldn't put my finger on it.

"You look good Meadow." She blushed and ate some of her food.

"What's up? Is everything ok?"

"Yea. I called you here because I wanted to tell you that I'm four and a half months pregnant and the baby is yours." When she said that the fork fell out of my hand and my mouth was hanging open. I knew the baby was mine but hearing she was carrying again had me happy as hell.

"Stand up." I told her and she did. She already had a small pouch.

"When did you find out?"

"The day I caught you at the bar. Gage, we may not be together but I would never hold news like this away from you again. I was mad and I'm sorry."

"I know baby. I was just asking that's all. Can I come to the next appointment?" I really shouldn't have to ask but I wanted to take things slow in getting her back. I saw everything Bruno went through winning Melina back and I was willing to go the same distance for Meadow.

"Yes. It's in a month away but the doctor is keeping a close eye on me due to the previous miscarriages." I sat there listening to her talk.

"Gage, I don't want to lose this baby. I need to know that if I need you for anything you will stop what you're doing and come running. If I lose this one I don't know what I would do." She started crying and I got up and sat next to her.

"Baby, I will move mountains for you if you wanted me to so of course I would stop what I'm doing to come to you. Don't cry Meadow. God is going to allow us to be parents this time I can feel it." I told her wiping her tears.

"Yea, but your brother and both of those women are out there and." I cut her off and kissed her. I didn't want her thinking anything bad and stressing herself out.

"Do you want me to come stay with you?" She nodded her head yes as she leaned back on my chest.

"I'll sleep in the guest room every night and leave the door open in case you need me. I know this doesn't mean we're back together but if this will keep your stress levels down I will do whatever it takes to keep you and my baby safe." She wiped her face and kissed my lips softly. My dick grew instantly and she started laughing.

"I hope you got tested after you slept with her." I reached in my wallet and pulled out my test results to show her. I went to the doctors the day after I slept with Hailey and got tested. I didn't know if Meadow would take me back and I'm still not sure but I knew that would be the first thing she asked.

"Meadow, I know you don't want to talk about it but I really am sorry. I never meant to hurt you. I was a weak nigga and should've had the strength to walk away. You are still the only woman I love and that will never change." I told her paying for our food. I helped her out the seat and walked her to the car. When we reached her car there was the word bitch in big letters spray-painted on the drivers' side and all her tires were flat. She just shook her head along with me.

"You coming back tonight right?" She asked getting in my car.

"Yup." Was all I said as I went to the hotel I was staying at and made three trips to my car with all my things. She tried to help me but I shut that shit down real fast. I didn't want her lifting, pulling or anything that may make her miscarry. Meadow was going to have this baby no matter what.

Chapter 8

Melina

71

Watching my sister's go through all this extra bullshit had a bitch thinking a lot about moving. I didn't want to move out of to state but just somewhere where all these ex's won't know where to find us. As you know I ain't no scary broad but after a while you grow up and don't want to deal with the drama. Bruno and I have been back together now for a few months. I gave him hell trying to win me back but he claims I was worth it and I can't say I disagree. The marriage proposal was more than any woman could wish for. It still doesn't bypass that the bitch claimed to be three months by him at the time. I thought that was odd because he told me they stopped messing around while he tried to win me back. You never really think about things people say when you're in that moment of arguing but when you have time on your hands the thought comes back up in your head.

He and I were in a good space right now but I still couldn't shake the feeling like he was still doing something on the side. I called his phone over and over all morning but it continued to go to voicemail. If anyone knows Bruno they know no matter where he is he won't turn his phone off now that his daughter Morgan is here. He is more over protective of her than anything and he always said he needed to be available at all times. I wasn't going to worry about it right now because as we all know if your man is cheating and he has a bitter bitch he's fucking she will come out and tell the main chick on purpose. Shana is definitely one of them so watching him with her right now at Babies r Us buy shit that he claimed wasn't going to happen until the child was born had me on a hundred.

"Hey guys. You must be shopping for the baby." They turned around and Bruno had a surprised look on his face and Shana of course was smirking. The real shocker was her turning around and having a stomach the size of Meadow's who was barely five months. If my memory served me correctly this chick should be eight if not nine months already.

"Ugh hey Melina." Bruno spoke first rubbing his head.

"Bruno, I've been trying to call you to see if you could pick some diapers up for Morgan since I was in class. I was finishing up my last semester in college. But I guess you needed to spend quality time with your other baby momma."

He pulled the phone out his clip and noticed it was off. I saw him power it back on and this chick was still grinning.

"Did you turn my phone off?" He asked her.

"Ugh yea. I didn't need her disturbing us again when you were making love to me." I saw Bruno's mouth hit the floor. Just like I thought; this bitch couldn't wait to tell me she's still been sleeping with him. We all know I could've beaten this bitch's ass but what for? He was still going to fuck with her and it was no use.

"Melina."

"I don't want to hear it. I'm just here to pick up some things for my daughter. You guys can finish shopping without worrying about me. How many months are you again Shana?" I could see Bruno sweating like a pig when I asked her that.

"Five months." I nodded my head.

"Oh I thought you were almost due by now."

"No. My first pregnancy was a false alarm. But now he and I can't wait. We just found out I was having his first son." I noticed how she threw first in there.

"Oh congratulations you two. It looks like you two are going to be spending a lot of time together now."

"What the fuck are you talking about Melina? We are about to get married." I laughed so hard in his face. He was crazy if he thought that was happening.

"Yea what are you talking about Bruno? I thought we were going to be together."

"What would make you think that Shana? Yea, I slept with you but you already know where my heart is and who I want to be with."

"But you said we could be together after I had the baby."

"Bitch, you're delusional. I never told you that." I listened to them go back and forth and walked over to the diaper section. I picked up diapers, lotion and a few other things for my baby. I stood in line waiting for the lady to ring me up. I felt his presence behind me but refused to turn around. My total came up to sixty dollars and he gave her his card. I kindly removed it from her hand and paid for my daughters' things.

"Stop being childish Melina. I can pay for Morgan's things." He said following me to my car. I put everything in my trunk and went to get in the car but he stopped me. The tears I held in started falling. He tried to wipe them but I backed away and got in my car.

"I'll meet you at the house." He said and I laughed. Bruno was really bugging if he thought I was going there. I was picking Morgan up from Maci and bouncing. I didn't even know where I was going but it was away from him.

"No need. You weren't worried about me or your daughter until you saw me."

"Melina you know dam well that's not true."

"Then you should've never been careless and allowed her to get that close to your phone to turn it off. Oh my bad you were making love to her as she says and I was always interrupting. How would you have felt if I was trying to get in touch with you because something happened to your daughter? You got caught slipping Bruno and this time I can honestly say you cheated and from the looks of it you have been for a while." I pulled my car off and left him standing there. I didn't need or want to hear his lame ass excuses. I wanted to move and there was no time like the present.

I got to Maci's house and she was outside in the back with Khalid and Morgan. Those two were trying hard to have another baby since she's been awake but it just wasn't happening yet. Khalid tried to tell her it was ok and when it was time it would happen but she wasn't trying to hear that. Anytime they were alone, she was sexing him up. Khalid was sitting behind Maci on one of the lawn chairs and Morgan was asleep on her chest. I couldn't wait for them to get married. I envied their relationship. Khalid was madly in love with my sister and vice versa. He never cheated on her and he never lied when he said another woman could get his attention if he was with someone.

"Hey you two." I slid the door open and sat next to them.

"What's wrong sis?" Maci could always tell when something was bothering us even if we sported a smile.

"Oh nothing. I found out Bruno was cheating on me and that the bitch is only five months pregnant with his son." I saw Khalid shake his head. He got up and took Morgan inside with him while we spoke. I broke down in front of my sister.

"Why do men cheat? I mean why when they have a good woman at home that does any and everything for him. Maci, there was nothing I wouldn't do for him. I took him back after all the other shit and he still couldn't keep his dick in his pants. I know it's not my sex game because I have his ass screaming like a bitch." She busted out laughing which made me laugh.

"I'm serious Maci. We see women who get cheated on and go back to men and that's their business but when you're the one dealing with it you see things from a different perspective. I know people out there wonder why it seems like black woman continue to go back to the man afterwards and honestly I can't answer that but for a biracial woman I can say it's probably the thought of them being with someone else that makes us stay. I can't even think about him satisfying another woman the way he does with me but I know he has because Shana gave me that information today."

"Melina, Bruno cheating doesn't mean that he doesn't love you or that he's not in love with you. It just means that he is an idiot and thinks with his dick. Women judge others all the time and that's the downfall of why we can't get along. Women are so busy trying to take the next baller from another woman but not realizing that a nigga won't wife her. Most men cheat just because they can but what these chicks need to realize that if he cheated with you, then he will do the same to them. Not only that; just about every man has a wifey/wife that he won't ever leave no matter how many side chicks or mistresses he has. Is it right no, but in this day and age these women don't have no respect for themselves and even appreciate being the side chick. It's crazy but it is what it is." I listened to my sister who is younger than me break it down like she's been dating forever.

"Why can't they be like Khalid?" She smiled and started rubbing my back.

"Melina, Khalid is a gift from God. I love that man with all my heart and I'm glad he picked me. I know there's temptation out there but he also knows what it is to lose me. I can't say what I would do because he makes it his business to never put me in that sort of position but if he did I would probably lose it. Listen sis, Bruno loves you we all know that but if you decide that he's not where you want to be then you have to let him go. You can't sit back waiting to see if he will change. If you decide to stay with him then let him see what he's missing before you take him back. Give him a taste of his own medicine and let him see how he feels."

"Maci, you're trying to get someone killed."

"I don't think he will kill you."

"No he will kill the guy. I can't have that on my conscience."

"So you're going to live your life unhappy? Why should he be allowed to mess around and you can't? You didn't whip Shana's ass like you could've. If you ask me you should let him feel the way you're feeling." I heard the door open and it was Khalid handing me Morgan who had a disgusting look on her face.

"Why she look like that?" I asked him before he went back in the house.

"Smell her and you tell me."

"Why your man just leave her like that?"

"Girl, he doesn't change shitty diapers yet."

"He better get ready because the way you two are going at it I'm sure it's about to happen." I saw her facial expression change. I took Morgan in to change her and Khalid was on his way out the door.

"I'll see you in a few babe." He told her and kissed her. She closed the door and plopped down beside me.

"What's up?" She broke down crying. I put Morgan on the floor after I changed her. Whatever was going on had my sister bawling her eyes out.

"You're scaring me sis. What's wrong?"

"It's a possibility I can't ever have kids." I covered my mouth and rubbed her back. I wanted to ask her how did she know but I waited for her to tell me.

"Aren't you going to ask me how I know?"

"I was waiting for you."

"When I was in the hospital and lost the first baby they did a DNC and cleaned me out. I had a clean bill of health but

81

whatever the nurse was injecting me with was killing my insides slowly. I don't know what else she was injecting me with but whatever it was I had allergic reactions too and that's why I had all those marks on my body. The only way I can have kids is if I try in vitro which may not work or adopt."

"Ok so what's wrong with that?"

"Khalid is going to leave me when he finds out."

"Girl bye. He isn't going anywhere. He loves the hell out of you and would let you adopt a thousand kids if that's what you wanted. Are you going to tell him?"

"I don't know how. He wants a baby so bad and I know this will break his heart."

"What about getting a surrogate to carry the baby for you?"

"HELL NO. Didn't you just see the preview for the movie where the man and his wife did that and the chick went crazy? That's a straight lifetime movie if you ask me." She and I both started laughing. I stayed over there for a while with my phone shut off. I didn't want to hear from Bruno plus I didn't want him to find me at this hotel I brought me and my daughter too. I opened my laptop and started looking for places to stay. I ran across a three-bedroom condo that was located fifteen minutes out of town and they were looking for someone to move in within the next month. Guess who was going to check the place out tomorrow? I sure was and I planned on asking the guy if I could move in sooner than later. I'm sure once I show up looking like money he won't have a problem.

Chapter 9

Bruno

I didn't plan on going to the store with Shana or even run into my girl while we were there. I saw the hurt on her face when Shana's stupid ass told her we slept together. I also noticed how Melina wouldn't allow a tear to drop in front of her. I think I was more shocked she didn't hook off on her but then again anyone could tell Shana was pregnant and that alone would've been a problem if the cops got involved. I raced to the house after I dropped Shana off but she wasn't there. I got a text from Khalid saying she was there and I felt a little better. I was going to go over there but he told me to meet him at the bar for a few drinks.

"What up bro?" I asked him and Gage who were sitting there chopping it up before I got there.

"Not much. What the hell is up with you and ole girl?" I told them what happened at the store and both of them shook their heads.

"How the hell is she only five months?"

"This bitch calls me up one day and ask me to come over because it was important. The possibility of her losing the baby was heavy on my mind since it could've been mine.

Anyway, I get there and the bitch offers me a few drinks that of course I watched her pour. She wasn't about to slip me anything." I saw them nod their heads. Women have been drugging niggas lately and that wasn't about to happen to me.

"I start feeling the effects of the alcohol and Melina was calling me. I told her if she didn't say what she wanted I was leaving. She tells me it was a false alarm and that she wasn't pregnant. I went to respond and the bitch was already on her knees sucking me off. Not too long after I found myself nutting in her. I didn't pay the shit no mind because I was rushing out to get back to Melina. Weeks went by and I hadn't heard from Shana and I was fine with that. Today the bitch calls and tells me this time she is pregnant. I go to her house and cursed her out. I felt like she tricked me into getting her pregnant. Well one thing led to another and I slept with her. I didn't realize she shut my phone off until I ran into Melina at the store and Shana couldn't wait to tell her I had just fucked her; well made love to her as Shana put it." I saw them with their mouths hanging open.

"Yo, you dumb as hell." Gage said and ordered another drink.

"I know you're not talking when Meadow caught your ass."

"Yea, but I admitted to my shit whether I was caught or not. I messed up but I know if she takes me back it won't happen again. Melina took you back after all that, accepted your proposal even after the bitch came and told her you were pregnant and you cheat on her with that exact woman who was there when she shot your tires out."

"I know man. Shana has been blowing my phone up since I dropped her off and Melina has her phone off."

"You know Shana got pregnant by you on purpose right?"

"You think so?"

"Yea dumb ass. She didn't get pregnant the first time and you went right over there and fucked her with no condom. She knew what she was doing; hell it was probably her ovulating time when she did it." I thought about what they said and ran my hand down my head. How could I be so fucking stupid? I deserve whatever Melina was about to do. But if she thought for one minute she was going to be with someone else she was sadly mistaken.

It's been three days since that mess happened with Melina and I haven't seen her. I was sick without her and it was my fault. Khalid told me her and Maci were going furniture shopping today for her new place. I was livid when he told me that because I thought she was coming back home. I threw my clothes on and went over to the place I knew she was buying from. I sat in the car watching her walk in the store picking things through the glass window. I couldn't help but notice how sad Maci looked. I was going to question my boy about that. Those two were never having problems and I know he wasn't cheating.

"You good Maci." I asked her when she walked out by herself. I saw the shocked look on her face.

"Yea, I'm good. What are you doing here?"

"I came to get my girl back." She shook her head and got in the car.

"Hey Bruno." Melina said smiling on her way to the car. She was texting someone on her phone that had her cheesing from ear to ear. I know dam well she wasn't fucking with someone already.

"Can we talk?"

"Sure. What's up?" She put her phone away and stood there staring at me. I looked at her and realized I fucked up. Melina was beautiful both inside and out and I fucked her over for some dumb bitch.

"Why are you staring at me? Say what you need to say." She had her arms crossed.

"Melina I want you to come home."

"Hell no. We are not about to have this conversation. Bruno you made it more than clear to me where you wanted to be."

"Melina, you know where I want to be. Why are you acting like that? Bring your ass home with my daughter." I was getting pissed.

"Fuck you nigga. Who the fuck do you think you are? You leave me to go screw some other chick and really get her pregnant this time and you think I'm going to stick around. Now who's delusional?" She went to open the car door and I stopped her.

"I fucked up ok. But you living somewhere else is not happening."

"Too late Bruno. You made your bed now lie in it. I'm sure you have more than enough bitches to help you stay warm at night. Oh, Morgan is at your parents' house."

"Hold up. You're out here buying new shit for a house you won't be staying in and my daughter is now less important to you." I regretted saying it as soon as it left my mouth. Melina started hooking off and screaming at me. I know the pain was more than me saying that and I let her get that until she smacked me a few times in the face. I grabbed her wrist and tossed her ass in my car. I gave her a look that dared her to get out.

"Go home Maci. I got her." She looked skeptical to leave but I could care less. I pulled up to my house and yanked her out the car. She stood their pouting with her arms crossed. I

89

carried her ass upstairs to the room and stripped her down to her birthday suit.

"Bruno, stop." She tried to fight me as I kissed her. My hand found its way to her treasure and caressed it until she came over my hands. I laid her down and made love to her. I couldn't fathom life without her and I know sex doesn't fix everything but the way her body responded to me showed that she was still mine.

"I love you Melina. I'm sorry." I wiped the tears that she let fall freely in front of me.

"Why?"

"Why what?"

"Why do you keep cheating?" I sat up and told her what happened.

"That's still not a reason to cheat. I'm tired of hearing about how men are doing something and the woman dropped down and gave him head that he couldn't walk away from. The bitch still has to get your clothes down before anything can happen. At that moment you should've gotten up and left. Yea, your dick may have been hard but you would've still had me."

90

she said and rolled over on her side. I never thought about how much it would hurt her from me sleeping with someone else. I was being selfish as hell and now I had to watch my girl cry tears over me again.

"I still have you Melina. You're mad and hurt right now and I understand. But there's no way on this earth that you will be with anyone else but me." She hopped up off the bed and started getting dressed.

"Fuck you. I'm tired of niggas saying a woman is his and she can't leave him. You should've thought about that before you cheated. You giving what was supposed to be my dick away but my pussy has to stay on lock. Nah, nigga. I'm going to explore what else is out there." I lit my blunt and walked over to her. I stood behind her and put my arm around her neck like I was choking her. I pulled it back a little just for her to feel me.

"Melina, if you ever allow another man to sniff my pussy I will put a bullet in your head and Morgan will grow up with a single dad."

"But." I let my arm grip her neck a little tighter but she could still breathe fine.

"But nothing. You thought I was playing when I said we were getting married and no other man better not touch you. I'm letting you know right now what will happen. Now fuck with it if you want."

"You would make my daughter motherless."

"Not on purpose. The decision is yours." I let her go and sat back down to smoke. She snatched her stuff up and walked out the room. I looked outside and she took the Audi. I didn't care she could drive anything she wanted it all belonged to her anyway she just didn't know it yet.

Chapter 10

Maribel

"Bitch if that nigga finds out I did that to his chick I'm a dead woman. When are you going to have the money so I can bounce?" I listened to my cousin go on and on about how she was scared of my ex. Yea, my cousin was the nurse who watched over that stupid bitch Maci. Every time Maci woke up I had her inject small amounts of cyanide to make her stay asleep. She also stuck some other shit in the IV to fuck up her insides. I was surprised Khalid didn't recognize her. But with the red hair and contacts he probably didn't pay her any mind. That bitch was never having kids by my man. I got up off the couch and got dressed to go meet up with the dude I was sleeping with.

"Where are you going Maribel? Did you hear what I said? That nigga is going to kill me."

"Girl, he doesn't even know who you are?"

"Bitch, I told you a few days after his girl went home I got a call that he went to the hospital in an uproar looking for me. He pulled a gun out on the nurses and everything. That man knows what happened somehow, otherwise he wouldn't be looking for me." She was getting on my fucking nerves.

I drove down by the beach to meet up with the dude and discuss how I was going to get my man back and he was dead set on getting revenge on Gage. I don't know what he did being he helped in the past you would think he appreciated it but he didn't. I watched him get out his car and drooled when I looked at him. This man was fine as hell. He was tall, brown skinned with a beard that I appreciated tickling my pussy every time he went down. His hair was in waves and he had that sexy bottom crown thing going on that the men were sporting these days.

"You're looking good." He said as I stepped out in my skintight jeans and belly shirt. We went inside and ordered our food. We were talking when I noticed Maci sitting at the table with some man. He was fine as hell too. She was looking sad until he lifted her chin with his finger. I couldn't snap my phone fast enough. I watched him pay for the food and get up. He pulled her in and gave her hug that seemed harmless but I looked at it as more than that. Dude I was with was cracking up and saying he couldn't wait for me to show Khalid that photo.

"Me either. His perfect Maci just showed her true colors." He and I finished our food and left.

I sat in my car debating on when I would send the video to him. I drove by the club to see if his car was there and it wasn't. I figured he was home and what better time to send the video then when she got there. I rode by the house next and just like I suspected he was standing at the door waiting for her to get out the car. I pulled my phone out and hit send. I may not be there but the fact that I knew shit was about to go down was more than satisfying to me. I was going to pull off but my Facebook notifications popped up and I started scrolling through them. Imagine my surprise when I saw him come storming out and racing out the driveway. I followed him to the club and watched him walk in mad as hell. I waited a half hour before I stepped out and went in. oh this was going to be fun.

Chapter 11

Khalid

I was sitting in my home office when Bruno hit me up and told me something was up with Maci. She looked upset or sad when he saw her at the furniture store. I hung up and called him but it went to voicemail. I figured she was on her way home and just didn't answer. I went back to my office and after another thirty minutes she wasn't home and I called her again. I looked down at my phone and saw it was a picture message from Maribel. I wasn't going to open it being that she has been sending me nothing but nude photos of herself. Another message came through and it was her saying I needed to keep a better eye on my fiancé. That made me open it up and to say I was upset was no way how I was feeling. I heard her car pull up and went rushing to the door. She walked up and smiled at me and tried to kiss me but I backed up.

"What's wrong?" I shut the door and stared at her.

"Are you cheating on me?" I asked and she seemed shocked that I would ask her something like that.

"Khalid, are you serious right now?" She put her purse and keys down and walked towards the kitchen.

"Where were you and why didn't you answer the phone when I called?" She turned around and put her hands on her hips.

"When did you start questioning me like a kid?"

"Don't change the subject. Where were you Maci?"

"I went out to lunch." I felt a little better that she didn't lie about that.

"With who?" I saw her swallow hard before she answered.

"Ok. Since you don't want to answer let me help you remember." I showed her the photos of her and the guy eating and the one of him hugging her. No words left her mouth as she stood there with tears falling down her eyes.

"Khalid wait." She grabbed on my shirt as I put my hand on the doorknob.

"I had lunch with the fertility doctor." I stopped and looked at her.

"What do you need a fertility doctor for?" She explained how whoever did this to her messed her body up and now she couldn't have kids without the help of in vitro or adoption.

"My problem with that is you being out on a date with another man and then allowing him to touch you. Not only that you didn't even come to me and let me know what was going on. I am your man but you forgot about that while you were smiling in another man's face."

"Khalid, he was just comforting me after we talked about me starting the in vitro."

"Are you fucking serious Maci? What fucking doctor goes out on a date to tell her something that should be done in the doctors' office? Huh? And then you letting that nigga put his hands on you like I don't fucking matter. How the fuck did you two even meet up to have a date?"

"He called me earlier and asked if I was available to meet him and that happened to be the place."

"Listen to yourself Maci. No doctor does that."

"Khalid, we were just talking."

"Just talking huh? Well maybe you should go find him so you can finish talking because what you should've been discussing with your man; no your fiancé about a baby, you do it with another man."

"Khalid you're not my fucking boss. I can go wherever I want and I don't need your permission."

"You are absolutely right. You're grown and can do what you want. Get the fuck out Maci." She spun around and looked at me.

"What?"

"Don't what me? You don't respect me or this relationship"

"What are you talking about?"

"This is the second time you have allowed some nigga to get in your ear and have you coming at me sideways. All I tried and wanted to do was love you but you're so busy trying to prove a point about you being grown you can't even see when a man is using you to get in between your legs. But hey

99

if that's what you want be my guest. I'm done trying to love you and make you see that no other man can love you the way I can."

"What are you saying?"

"I'm saying it's over. I'm done playing these games with you. It's clear that you were too young for what I wanted to build with you. I get it. You want to experience other things and men so I'm letting you go to do just that."

"You're being dramatic and I'm not going anywhere." I stepped in front of her and made sure I spoke with enough authority that she knew not to test me.

"Maci, I don't know who the fuck you think you're talking to but let's get one thing straight. I run shit and the faster you realize it the better. I'm going out and you better be long gone before I return or you'll be dragged out of here by your hair like that bitch was in that Madea movie. Fuck with me if you want."

"You would do that to me."

"Get the fuck out my face." I slammed the door and I heard her yell something but I just kept going. I sped to my

club because I needed a drink to calm me down from fucking
her up and finding out who this doctor dude was. I tossed shot
after shot back when I noticed my stupid ass ex come strolling
in. I can admit she was looking good but I wasn't about to go
there or at least I thought I wasn't. She sat next to me in the
VIP section and started running her hands up and down my
pole. I moved her hand away multiple times but she kept
putting them back making my man harder.

"Let me make you feel good K." That's what she
always called me when we were about to have sex. Her tongue
was in my ear as she unbuttoned my jeans and put her hands in.
There weren't a lot of people in the club and it was dark as hell
in my section. I usually have some sort of candles lit on the
table but since it was just me all I wanted to do was sit in the
dark. That was probably the best choice I made being as
though Maribel was sucking the hell out of my dick. It felt so
good but all I could think of was Maci. Technically I wasn't
cheating on her because I told her it was over and to move out
so there was no guilt. I just wished it were her doing it instead.

"Shit Maribel. You're definitely making me feel good."

101

"Mmmmm. You taste just like I remember." I watched her suck me dry and jerk me again to get hard.

"Can I feel you inside me?" Before I got to answer she was sliding down on my dick and wetting me the hell up. She always did know how to ride a good dick. She went up and down, in circles and lifted her legs on my shoulders while she did it.

"Damn girl. This pussy still good."

"You know it. I'm sorry about everything that happened between us. I miss you K. Fuck, I'm ready to cum." I heard what she said and didn't respond. I still wasn't taking her back no matter how good she had me feeling. I watched her body convulse as she came hard. I lifted her up and bent her over the banister that looked down on the dance floor. It looks like we were watching people dance but I was digging deep in those guts. If the music wasn't so loud one could hear how loud she was screaming.

"Throw that ass back Maribel." She started doing it and my nut was coming up quick. Her ass was juggling and the sight of me going in and out was driving me in sane. She moved back and I fell on the couch with her now riding me cowgirl style. I went to lift her up and she bounced harder and we both came at the same time with me releasing my babies in her.

"Shit K. I've never had anyone fuck me like you."

"You never will either. Get up so I can go clean up." I smacked her ass and watched her put her clothes back on. I pulled my clothes up and went into my office to clean myself off.

"Was it worth it?" I heard when I came out the bathroom.

"Yup. It sure was."

"I thought you said you weren't a cheater." Maci said standing there looking out the glass down at the crowd.

"Oh I'm not. You see I told you it was over before I left. I gave you the freedom you were looking for."

"I didn't want any freedom. I thought about what you said and you were right. I should've never gone out on a date with another man regardless if it was a doctor. I know you had my best interest at heart and were looking out for me. I'm sorry for making you look like a fool but I guess we're even now because that's exactly what you did to me." She said and picked her purse up to leave.

"Maci, I think it's best if we stay away from each other. You are obviously looking for something I can't give you and I don't want to have this conversation again down the road because you don't want me to check you when you're wrong. I will always love you but us being together is not in our future." I saw her wiping her eyes as she grabbed on the doorknob.

"Hey Maci." I heard Maribel say when she opened the door and moved past her.

"That was quick Khalid but I heard you loud and clear."

"K, I don't know if I got all the cum you left in me out. Can I take a shower in there please?" I was fucked up when she said that. Maci's mouth hit the floor and I saw her run out. I wanted to punch my ex in the face but it was my fault for fucking her. I knew how she got down and this was probably making her day. I went to run behind Maci and didn't have to go far. She was sitting on the floor outside my office breaking down and crying harder than she was before she left. I leaned up against the wall and laid my head back. She sat there for about five minutes and the shit tore me up on the inside.

"I guess now that you found out I couldn't have kids you go and nut in the first chick you fuck." She stood up, wiped her face and fixed her clothes.

"I messed up but it had nothing to do with your situation. You know I don't want any kids with her." She scoffed up a laugh and started walking away.

"Maci." I grabbed her arm.

"No Khalid. You told me it was over but I came here to beg you to take me back. I was hurt by the way you spoke to me but I understood everything you said. I didn't like you being disrespectful to me but I got it. I couldn't find you so I went to your office only to walk past VIP and see you screwing your ex. I stayed because I know you probably acted on impulse. But to hear you didn't even use a condom and will most likely end up with a baby by her because that's what she wants is making my heart hurt so bad. It feels like someone is stabbing me over and over in it. But I understand that we are no longer together. I hope you have fun raising a kid with a woman who doesn't give a shit about her other one but desperately doing everything to have one with you."

"Maci."

"Bye Khalid. Give me a couple of hours and I'll be out of your life forever."

"Maci. Maci." I yelled out but she kept walking. I went back in and Maribel was sitting on the couch naked.

"Put your clothes on." She looked shocked.

"Don't tell me you're upset about the break up? Come on let's finish what we started."

"Just go Maribel. If I need to hit you up I will. And you better get a plan b pill."

"What? I'm not taking that shit." She said and left out the office. I wasn't worried about that because I was taking it to her. I may not be with Maci but I damn sure ain't about to have kids with that crazy bitch ex of mine either.

Chapter 12

Maci

I ran down the steps to the club so fast I didn't realize I was out the door and in the middle of the street about to get hit until I felt someone grab me. I looked up and it was Dr. Stanton. The one who I went to lunch with and told me to start the in vitro shots. He pulled me to the side and asked me if I was ok. I heard him tell his boys that he would catch up with them in a few. I can't lie and say this man wasn't turning me on because he was. He had on some dark black jeans with a white thermo shirt and some wheat timbs. He wore a necklace that was shining bright and he had an earring in one of his ears. If I didn't know he was a doctor I would've assumed drug dealer off the back.

"I'm sorry I guess I wasn't paying attention." He lifted my chin.

"Don't apologize beautiful. I will save you anytime." He said and kissed my cheek before stepping off. I thought about what Khalid said and it dawned on me that this man did want me and I was too stupid to see it. I opened my car door and drove over to the house to get my things. Melina was coming to help me because Meadow was pregnant and Gage wasn't allowing her to go anywhere without him. Morgan was with my parents because my dad's mom was visiting from up north and wanted to spend every second with her.

"Come on bitch. I don't want to be here when he gets back." I yelled out at Melina who was boo loving with her new friend on the phone. He wanted to come with her but she and I both knew that was a bad idea. I packed up a few of my toiletries, my underclothes, my school supplies and some other things. All the clothes, shoes and purses he brought that I didn't wear he could keep. I didn't need anything from him and he could give it to the next bitch. I know it sounds crazy but I was willing to overlook the cheating part but once that bitch said he came in her I was over it. My heart was broke and Khalid was the person who did it.

"Bitch, you still didn't tell me what happened and why you moved out." Melina said handing me a glass of wine. I told her what happened and she sat there listening without judging me. She put her glass on the coaster and sat back to look at me.

"First off Maci, you were wrong in all aspects of what happened. How do you get mad at your fiancé for checking you about being out with another man? Another man that you just found out wants you. Then you tell him he can't tell you what to do which I get but why did you feel like he was doing that when it was clear that you were deceiving him by not telling him about you and your situation. Maci, you never vent to another man about your home life whether he wants you or not. That is how they prey on women."

"I know but I didn't know he looked at me like that and I was just trying to figure out how to tell Khalid without him leaving me."

"Bullshit Maci. Khalid would not have left you for something like that. You were trying to boss up on him and his ass had to bring you down a notch. He's not like other men Maci; hell none of them are. They crazy as hell but they mean well and just don't know how to show it."

"Ok, so I'm supposed to accept that he cheated?"

"Girl bye. He told you it was over before he left. Yes, it may have been an hour or so later that you saw him screwing another woman but at the end of the day he didn't cheat. You can see it the way you want but you know I'm right. I admit he went about it wrong and could've waited or not had sex in the club but you weren't together." I don't know if I should be mad at Melina for taking his side or what but I wasn't feeling her at this moment. I stood up to leave and go in my room. I was now staying with her instead of getting a place of my own.

"Maci, I know this is all new to you but when you're in a relationship its no longer just you. You have to talk to your man and make decisions together. You are your own woman but he was right no doctor will ask you to meet him for lunch to discuss personal business like that. You were clearly on a date with another man whether you saw it like that or not. You would've had a fit if the roles were reversed and you know it." I grinned and looked down at my phone that was vibrating. It was my ex sending me a message.

Khalid- *You left some things here.*

Me- *No I didn't. Whatever is left you can give to your new bitch since she tried everything to be me and you finally let her. I can afford my own shit. Everything that's still there is because I don't need it just like I don't need you. Good-bye Khalid.* My phone started ringing from him. I waited for him to stop calling and picked it up to call Verizon and have it changed. I was happy that they did it right away because I could see me answering it if he continued calling.

The next few weeks flew by and it was Meadow's baby shower. She made it to eight and a half months and we were ecstatic. They found out she was having a boy and my dad couldn't wait until he got here. Melina and I threw the shower at my parents' house because my grandparents on my dad side and my evil ass aunt were coming. Meadow didn't want my aunt to know where she lived or how nice she had it. She was always looking for a handout.

"Everything looks good ladies." My dad said and picked up a stuffed mushroom off the tray. We had the food catered and hired a DJ too. The backyard was huge and we decorated it blue and white. Meadow came strolling in at exactly two when it was supposed to start. She had on a long white dress with a white flower sticking out her heads. Her hair was going straight down her back and her makeup was flawless. The minute Gage walked in he was all over her. They hadn't gotten back together yet but he was trying his hardest to win her over.

"You look good Melina." I heard Bruno say and she rolled her eyes and walked out. These men killed me with their *"I can do what I want with whoever but you can't"* attitudes. I heard the voice of the man I didn't want to and tried to run out the room. I went one way as I heard him walking in the other. I knew I wouldn't be able to avoid him for the entire party but I needed to prepare myself. I started hyperventilating and my anxiety was at an all-time high. I wasn't over him but I could no longer be with him either and he made that clear twice that night. A half hour later I got myself together and went to go downstairs. I had my hair up in a ponytail that allowed my hair to hang down my back. My jeans were a little tight and my shirt only covered my breast. I had a necklace around my waist that connected to my belly ring. I threw some more lip-gloss on with my shades and walked out the door.

"Damn. All three sisters are fine." I heard some guy say. I grinned and went on to introduce myself to the people I didn't know.

"You look gorgeous Maci." His breath could be felt on the back of my neck and his cologne was over powering my vanilla scent. I wanted to turn around but I was being childish and moved away from him.

"Bitch, why is Khalid and Bruno drooling over the two of you?" Meadow said laughing and eating some food.

"I guess they're realizing what they lost out on." Melina said and we slapped high fives. The shower went on and my sister got so many things and a lot of money. Melina and I ended up going out to the car to smoke a blunt. This wasn't something we usually did but the guy Melina was fucking with had us try some one-day and the shit was good. It had me relaxed and in a zone which is what I needed right now. I heard her suck her teeth and when I looked Bruno was coming to the car.

"When did you start smoking?" He pulled her out the car and she started laughing. I guess her high was already kicking in because she would've been arguing with him for that. I could hear him going back and forth with her about being on some dumb shit and she just kept laughing. She really pissed him off when she told him somebody else had her attention. I swore I saw fire come from the top of his head. I jumped out the car and ran to where she was but was snatched up by none other than my ex.

"Is it snatch up your ex day today or something? What the fuck you want?" I tried to get out of Khalid's grip but he wasn't letting go. He walked me down the street to where his car was and pushed me against it. His lips found mine but I wouldn't let him gain access inside with his tongue. I held out as long as I could until he found the spot on my neck and I let out a moan. He forced his tongue to dance with mine and I felt myself dripping wet down there.

"Khalid shit."

"I love you Maci." I wanted to say something but he was moving my pants down my legs. I stepped out of one leg and he plunged deep inside my wetness with no remorse. I yelled out because it's been awhile but the euphoric feeling took over as I came. He laid me back on the hood of the car and slowly grinded in and out of me. My eyes were rolling in my head once again from another orgasm. His hands were massaging my chest and he was sucking the hell out of them. He pulled me off the car and made me bend over while he dog fucked the hell out of me.

"Maci, this is still mine. Damn, I can't hold out any longer. Fuckkkkk baby. Shit. Got damn." He released himself in me and I was mad. He wasn't my man and I don't know who else he had been sleeping with. He lifted me up and helped me put my clothes back on while he did the same. The street was dark but a car came creeping up the street and he told me to get in the car and hit the floor. He was still standing out there with his gun in his hand waiting. I heard him yell what the fuck does she want and that made me look up.

"How much longer are you going to be here?"

"Maribel, how did you find me? Never mind why are you questioning me?" I was going to get out but I wanted to hear what she was going to say.

"Khalid, you said you would think about us getting back together but how can you do that when you're here at your ex's family house. I know she's in there."

"First off don't worry about where she is and second my brother is having a baby by her sister. What type of shit you on?"

"Ok. But you're telling me that you haven't spoken to her."

"Nah. She's not talking to me and I aint fucking with her like that." The minute he said that he looked over at the car to see if I was looking out but I ducked down.

"Take your ass home and I'll be there in a few."

"Why can't I come to your house?"

"You will never come to my house unless you're my girl and right now you're not."

"I better not find out you with that bitch." He yanked her up.

"Don't call her a bitch. Now take your stupid ass home." I heard her pull off and I jumped out the car and was speed walking to the door.

"Get the fuck off me Khalid. I hate you." He let go and stared at me.

"You hate me."

"I fucking hate you. How dare you allow that bitch to find out where my parents live and then you tell her you not fucking with me like that? Nigga, I just fucked you out here and you're denying me like I'm some jump off. Oh that's because I am. How could I be so stupid and fall victim to your ass again?"

"Maci, I didn't want her to cause a scene."

"Cause a scene. You mean like us screwing outside could've caused one. Khalid, the shower is over and Gage left with my sister. I think the best thing for you to do is bounce. Your girl is home waiting for you." I slammed the door in his face and went to my old room, hopped in the shower then cried myself to sleep.

Chapter 13

Meadow

Today was my last visit to the doctors before I gave birth to my son. I wanted to make him a junior but Gage refused to give our son his name. He claimed it was cursed with all the bad luck he had over the last year. The doctor told us I was two centimeters and I should be giving birth within the next few days if I kept dilating. Gage was happy as hell and I was too. We lost two babies and God blessed us again. We left out the doctors' office and I followed him to I hop because I was hungry as hell.

"Hello. Welcome to Ihop what can I get for you guys?" The waiter asked. He took our orders and came back a few minutes later with our drinks.

"Are you ready babe?"

"I don't know Gage. Everyday it's getting closer and closer to the due date. I want to have a natural birth with no meds but then again after watching the baby channel it looks painful."

"Whatever you decide I'll be there the entire time. If I haven't told you before I'm going to say it now."

"What?" She looked at me confused.

"Thank you for giving me a son."

"You're thanking me. I should be thanking you for squirting inside me and trusting me to carry your baby. I honestly didn't think I was going to make it." I felt my eyes getting watery.

"Meadow, what happened to you wasn't because of natural causes due to an issue with your body. We both know how you lost them and this time none of that even played a factor. I knew in my heart you would carry full term. God took our other two angels because he knew the atmosphere was fucked up at the time. Baby, you are going to deliver my son fine and if you let me I'm letting off more babies in you." I grinned and smacked his arm.

"I'm serious Meadow. I still want you to be my wife. Can a nigga come home?"

"You are home Gage."

"Yea, but I haven't had no pussy or been allowed to sleep in the same room as you."

"Yes baby you can come home. Mommy misses you too." He leaned over and kissed my lips and I felt butterflies in my stomach. I loved everything about him. He has been staying in the guest room and I wouldn't dare sleep with him. I hear him handling himself at night instead of going out to sleep with another woman but that's his fault. We finished our food and of course I took some food to go.

"I'm hopping in the shower Gage."

"Me too." He yelled from the guest room. When I got out he was standing there soaking wet with just a towel wrapped around him. He sat on the bed and moved me closer to him and kissed my stomach.

"I love you Meadow."

"I love you too Gage." He lifted my leg on his shoulder and brought me so much pleasure he had to sit me down before I fell. I returned the favor and he was yelling out my name and gripping the sheets.

"I guess the saying is true about pregnant pussy being the best. Baby, it's so good I don't ever want to cum."

"Shit Gage. I'm cumming again."

"I'm serious Meadow. I may keep you pregnant just to have this feeling." He had me turn over and the sounds from him going in and out had me releasing again.

"I'm cumming baby. Ahhh shitttt Meadow." His body fell on the bed next to mine and I could hear him trying to catch his breath.

"Let me know when you're ready for round two." He said smacking my leg and getting a washcloth to clean us off.

"Whenever you are. You say my pussy is good well baby that dick is the bomb and it's needed inside me right now."

"Say no more." He sexed me off and on all night. I think we fell asleep after two in the morning. It was well worth it; that for sure.

****

Six weeks ago I gave birth to a healthy baby boy and Gage did what he said and was there the entire time. Today

121

was my checkup at the gynecologist since I gave birth. I had him put me on birth control pills once I had my son and I didn't slip up having sex before he told me they would work. Oh I was giving my man more kids but not right now. He understood and didn't fight me on it even though I know he wanted to. He wasn't trying to get on my bad side ever again.

I pulled into the driveway after I put my code in and saw a small but new Honda accord. I never saw the car before and when I looked inside of it, it looked brand new. I opened the door and was greeted by a smell of food. I was hungry too; I couldn't wait to see who was cooking and what it was. I stepped closer in my kitchen and stopped the moment I saw her. She had my son in her arms while she fed him a bottle with something red in it. My son was choking but she continued to force the bottle in his mouth. I ran over and snatched my Javion out her hands and told her to get the fuck out.

"I don't have to go anywhere. This is my son's house." I looked down at my son who was still coughing and saw he was turning blue. I called 911 and told them I needed assistance because my son wasn't breathing. The EMT's got there in no time and started performing CPR on him. His skin was red like whatever was in the bottle gave him and allergic reaction. I lifted the top off the bottle and the shit had straight up hot sauce in it. I ran in the kitchen to beat her ass when I felt a strong pair of arms grab me.

"Ma'am if you hit her I will have to arrest you for assault."

"You need to arrest her because she was feeding my son a bottle of hot sauce." The officer looked at me then over at her.

"Is that true ma'am?"

"Why would I feed my grandson hot sauce? I think you should take her down to be checked because she is crazy. You saw she tried to attack me." The bitch said and I tried to get her again. A female officer came in and told me this was the last time they were telling me to calm down.

"Where's the bottle?" She handed the officer a bottle.

"It smells like dish soap ma'am."

"That's because she rinsed it out. Get the fuck out of my house now."

"What is going on?" Gage came running in with Bruno behind him. I told him what happened but when he asked his mom she lied.

"Ma'am do you still want her to leave the officer asked me?"

"Yes."

"Like I said this is my son's house."

"Bitch go."

"Meadow, hold on. I don't appreciate you talking to my mom like that."

"Nigga you can take you and your mom and get the fuck out. You forgot that everything in this bitch is mine. I suggest you leave before I have these nice officers escort you out."

"Are you serious Meadow?" I saw more officers walking in.

"Dead fucking serious. If you'll excuse me I have to go to the hospital and make sure my son didn't die because you let the same woman who allowed her son, your brother to almost rape me watch my kid. The kid of a woman she can't stand.

Officer can you please make sure they leave the property?"

The officers nodded. When I got to my car the female officer came over to me.

"Meadow. If I can call you that."

"Yes." I was wiping the tears from my eyes.

"Let me take you to the hospital. You are in no position to drive." I stepped out the car and got in with her. I saw the officers walking out with Gage and his mom.

"Meadow, I understand what you are going through but as a mother myself you have to control yourself or you're going to end up in jail and that woman will be able to really harm your kid." I shot a look at her.

"You believe me don't you?"

"Yes. When I smelled inside the bottle there was a small stench of hot sauce lingering."

"Why didn't you say something?"

"Meadow, I'm new to the force. Well just new to this area. I've only been her maybe seven months. I came from up north where my husband who was a detective was killed in the line of duty. I couldn't take going to work every day and people giving me the sympathy look. I asked for a transfer and this is where they put me. The guy you have a son with is a very powerful man. He and two other guys basically have the force under wraps. You see I'm new and I think I will be receiving a visit from them very soon."

"Why do you say that?"

"Because I wasn't supposed to offer to have them escorted off the premises. One of the other officers told me before I came in to stay out of it but me being who I am refused. Once I smelled the bottle I wanted that woman out of your house just as fast."

"I don't know what I'm going to do. I love Gage but I can't have his mom around my son."

"Then don't allow it. If you have to get a restraining order on her then do it. I'm tight with one of the judges that can't be bought and she will sign off on it. But know if you do it there will be consequences."

"I'm not worried about him doing anything to me." I said proudly and got out the car. She rolled her window down.

"Be careful because those men run this town, county and probably entire state. You don't know who knows who so keep your business to yourself and trust no one." I shook my head and ran inside the emergency room to find my baby. The doctors were looking over him when I got there and asked to speak to me in the hallway. I saw a woman dressed in slacks coming towards us with a folder in her hand. She introduced herself as someone from child protective services and extended her hand. My parents walked in with Maci and Melina right behind them. I knew all hell was going to break loose when Gage came with a scowl on his face.

"Come here Meadow."

"I can't Gage because I have to sit here and explain why your son had an allergic reaction to hot sauce when he is way too young to have it." The look on his face was priceless.

"Who was watching your son when he drank it?"

"His mother." Call me a snitch all you want but that bitch needs to go to jail.

"His grandmother."

"Fuck that bitch. She tried to kill your son and you're sitting here trying to give her ass a title."

"Gage, I think you need to leave." My dad said standing up. I saw Gage walking towards him and me and my sisters stood up.

"Are you fucking serious right now? You're coming for my father over some shit your mother did."

"You don't know if my mother did that and your father can get it too." This has to be the worse day of my life right now. The man I loved defending his mom for trying to kill our son then trying to fight my dad for telling him to leave. My dad took his shirt off and got into a boxing stance. He caught Gage in the mouth and I thought that was it.

"Oh my God daddy. Why did you hit him?" I couldn't believe this was happening. I heard the hospital paging security. The entire scene was chaotic.

"You got that old man but just know your time is coming."

"Was that a threat?" I asked following him as he walked out the door.

"Take it how you want to take it but nobody and I mean nobody puts their hands on me and walks away to tell it." I smacked the fuck out of him.

"What the fuck is wrong with you? Where is my man Gage? The Gage I know would never allow his mom to harm his son or come for his wife. Well that's what he told me. Gage, I know you love your mother but I can't be with you if you're going to allow her to get away with this. You will always be our son's father but he won't ever be around you when she's there."

"Meadow, I want to see you try and stop me from seeing him."

"I didn't say you couldn't see him. I said he can't be around your mom and so did the lady from child protective services."

"That's because you put it in her head."

"Gage, I know it's hard for you to believe your mom would do this but I would never lie to you about something like that. I may not like her but I wouldn't blame her if I didn't see it with my own eyes." I saw his eyes getting glassy. I think he knew in his heart she did it but didn't want to believe it.

"I love you Meadow, but until you stop this nonsense about my mom we can't be together."

"I love you too Gage. I always will, but I won't deny to you or anyone else what I walked in on. Goodbye."

"Meadow take it back." He grabbed my arm.

"I wish I could Gage but I saw her."

"FUCK!" He yelled out and tossed a few chairs in the waiting room. I went back to where everyone was and waited for them to let me see my son. The lady came from the back and said Javion couldn't be around Gage or his mother until there was a full investigation. My life was spiraling out of control and there was nothing I could so to stop it.

Chapter 14

Gage

I stormed out the hospital when Meadow wouldn't take back what she said about my mom. I thought I was being nice by allowing my mother to come see her first grandson but I guess a zebra never changes its stripes. I don't know what it is that she has against Meadow or the fact that she evidently tried to kill my son. I would've lost it if anything happened to him and I know my girl would have too. It seems like we just can't catch a break. The minute things are going good there's bullshit lurking around the corner. I parked in front of my mom's house and got out. She was in there talking to my grandmother who I hadn't seen since she got out of jail. Yea my grandmother was in jail for a year for possession of a firearm. Her ass didn't have it registered and she had outstanding warrants for tickets so they made her do a year.

"Hey Gage." My grandmother stood up to give me a hug. I grabbed a water out the fridge and sat down. I stared at my mother to see if she felt bad or gave off any inclination that she did what Meadow said.

"What the fuck you staring at?" My mom barked at me and my grandmother looked up.

"Ma, please tell me you didn't try and kill my son." I saw my grandmother look at my mom and roll her eyes. Those two didn't have the best relationship but I knew my grandmother was waiting for her answer just like I was.

"Boy, don't nobody want to kill your kid. You need to take a blood test to see if he yours anyway. He looks more like your brother then you." I hopped up off that seat so quick and had my mom up by her shirt. I never disrespected her but saying some shit like that was about to get her killed. I could hear my grandmother in my ear telling me to let go.

"Did you try and kill my son?"

"Get off me Gage. What the hell is gotten into you?" I let her go and walked by the door.

"I'll tell you what got into you. It's that damn girl turning you against me and your brother."

"Grandson, I know you didn't let that happen." When she called me that it was because she was trying to keep me calm. I told her what happened. She had pure disgust on her face and my mother just sat there looking stupid.

"You know the vile things Jesse does, how could you let him try and rape his girl? What's wrong with you?" My grandmother got up and smacked my mother across the face. My mom stood up but she knew not to say shit. My grandmother wasn't anything to fuck with. In all of her fifty-three years she has never lost a fight and my mom knew it. I saw my mom start crying and I wanted to feel bad but I couldn't find it in my heart to.

"You allowed your brother to sit in jail for ten years while you were sitting at home doing whatever. How could you?" I finally heard my mom tell me what her real issue was with me. She blamed me for her son sitting in jail.

"Ma, we all saw on tape what he did to that woman. He raped her over and over and got away with it." She covered her ears and tried to act like she was singing.

"You're right I could've gotten him off with a slap on the wrist but he deserved that jail time. He needed to take time out and have remorse for what he did. Not only did he rape that woman but he instilled fear in her and took something away from her that he didn't get permission for. I thought him being in jail would have him come out a better man but ma he tried to rape my girl and you helped him. I love you but I can't come around anymore. You are slowly trying to make me lose everything I'm trying to build with my girl."

"You see. I told you she was taking you away from us."

"No she isn't ma, you are. That woman has done nothing to make you dislike her; yet, you treat her like shit. I brought you to my house to meet your first grandson and to get to know her and look what happened."

"I didn't do anything. And what does that have to do with me."

"I CAN'T EVEN SEE MY SON BECAUSE THEY CALLED THE PEOPLE ON HER. THEY ALMOST TOOK HIM AWAY FROM HER AND FOR WHAT? ME TRUSTING YOU TO GET TO KNOW HER AND MY SON." I slammed my hand on the table and got up. I heard the front door swing open and before I could react, Meadow was punching my mom in the face. My grandmother looked at me and I put my hand up for her not to jump in it. This was something Meadow had to do; hell if that weren't my mom I would do it. My mom was able to get a few hits in but my girl was putting a hurting on her. I saw Maci and Melina run in along with their mom. Everyone just stood there and let my girl whoop on my mom.

"I better not ever see you on my side of town. Every time I see you I'm going to whoop your ass." I grabbed Meadow off my mom and had her against the wall. My grandmother offered everyone a seat, which shocked the hell out of me. When my mom stood up she had blood coming from her nose, mouth and forehead. I checked Meadow over and she started crying. I moved her hair behind her ear and kissed her tears.

"Don't cry baby. It's over now. She won't be around our son or you."

"I love you Gage." She put her arms around my neck.

"I love you too baby. Where's my son?"

"With my dad."

"Let's go get him. I need to holler at your pops."

"Not today Gage. He is still mad and I know you are too." I told her we could do it another day.

"Damn, that girl whooped your ass." My grandmother said to my mom when she came out the bathroom.

"She may have whooped my ass but I will have the last laugh. You took my son Gage away from me and my other son can't show his face because his brother wants him dead." She pointed a gun at Meadows head and everyone started screaming except Meadow.

"You allowed your son to almost rape me and I was still willing to try and be cordial with you on the strength of Gage and my son. Then you try and kill my son and are now pulling a gun on me. I'm telling you right now you better kill me because I am going to beat the fuck out of you if you don't. I've never done anything for you to have so much hate towards me but you can bet that this isn't over." Meadow walked up to her and put the gun to her head. My mom's hands were shaking. I ran over and took that shit from my mom. The look on my girls face was serious. It was like she was another person but I guess when someone pulls a gun out on you that

136

will do it. Melina was pulling Meadow out but she stood there waiting for me.

"Gage, if you leave with her you can forget that I'm your mother. I will disown you."

"How the fuck you going to disown your son for the fucked up shit you did? Shut the fuck up and take that ass whooping like a champ. You lucky she didn't snatch that gun out your hand and shoot you." My grandmother was going in on my mom but the words that she said was not only hurtful but made me realize that she had no love left for me.

"You will always be my mother and if you're choosing your son the rapist and hatred over me then I guess I'll see you when I see you. This is my girl, my son's mother, my soon to be wife. If you think I'm leaving her behind some foul shit you've been doing you're crazier than I thought. Grandma here's my number and I would love for you to meet your great grandson." I kissed both of them on the cheek and picked Meadow up and walked out the door. She was still in shock about my mom pulling a gun out on her. I parked in the driveway and made sure the gate was closed and the house was locked up. My son was staying with her parents for the night. I started a bath for her, stripped her clothes off and placed her in the tub with me sitting behind her.

"Today has been an eventful day." That was the first time she spoke since we left my mom's house. I massaged her shoulders and felt her starting to relax. She turned her body around to face me and used her hands to get me hard. When she did I helped guide her down on my dick and let her ride me until we both released. It was like we both needed it because we were more relaxed afterwards. After we washed up I helped her out and we made love throughout the night.

"Meadow, I'm sorry that my family is causing so many problems."

"It's not your fault. I'm just glad you believe me this time. I love you so much Gage. If you didn't I don't think we could've ever been together and I would've questioned the love you claim to have for me?"

"Meadow, I love you more than you will ever know." I kissed her lips and we both fell asleep holding one another.

****

I woke up early the next day and went into the office we had downstairs and pulled up the cameras. I believed Meadow but I had to see it for myself. I rewound the footage to yesterday. I had a few tears running down my face as I watched my mom pour hot sauce in my sons' bottle and try to feed him. Right before my girl walked in she took a vial out her pocket and poured it in the pot. Whatever it was, was probably to kill my girl. She had it out bad for Meadow. I felt her massaging my shoulders as she kissed on my neck.

"I'm sorry Meadow. I thought I was doing something good by inviting her here to work it out with you and meet my son."

"It's ok baby. I know it's hard seeing your mom try to get rid of us."

"It is but I know you wouldn't lie about it. I was mad that the cops were involved."

"Gage, when you call the ambulance the cops always come? Its protocol." She sat on my lap and watched the video with me.

"Baby turn that up." I said. She hit the button for the volume and I heard my mom discussing some dangerous shit. She told the person on the phone about the gate to my house and how it will be hard to pass it. She also told the person Meadow was set to come home at any time and they should be at the gate waiting for her. I couldn't believe the things she was saying or that she was trying to set us up.

"Get up Meadow."

"No. Gage I know you're mad but going over there is not a good idea."

"Meadow, she wants you and my son dead. Did you not hear her say she was about to set me up? Mother or not she has to go." She stood up and stripped in front of me and my dick tried to break free immediately. My girl had a badass body and could get me hard but just showing me her stomach.

"You think you slick."

"Who me?" She put her hands up and I snatched her panties off and devoured her pussy like I was in a pie-eating contest.

"Fuck Gage. This dick is so good."

"How good baby?" I was pumping in and out of her.

"Real good. Here I cum baby."

"That's my girl. Wet it up." I came not too long after her. After we washed up she stayed up under me all day to make sure I didn't leave. That's ok. I could stay home today but tomorrow was another day and my mother better hope I'm in a good mood.

Chapter 15

Khalid

I really fucked up with Maci this time. The night I slept

with Maribel at the club I messed around and hit her off a few more times after that. I know I said I would never do it again but I didn't want to go sleep with any random chicks and since she was available I just did it. I would only fuck her in a hotel room and never my house. Even though I told Maci to leave I would never allow another woman in there to sleep in her bed. Of course I had to hear Maribel whine about wanting to wake up to me and have breakfast in bed. I let her know she was only a fuck and there was no feelings involved whatsoever. I was getting ready to go by Gage's house to see my nephew when I got a text message from Maribel asking me to meet her at some address because it was an emergency.

I didn't want to go but fuck it. I pulled into this little spot that looked like a house and text her I was outside. She came out and dragged me in. I saw a few women sitting in what looks like a waiting room at a doctor's office. She told the nurse she was ready to go back in the room and me like an idiot still had no idea what was going on.

"Good morning. Are you ready to see your baby?" The doctor asked and I damn near passed the fuck out.

"Come again." I said making sure I heard him correctly.

"You, well she is pregnant and were about to see how far along she is." Dude looked mad familiar but I couldn't figure it out. He had Maribel get undressed and squirted some gel on some tube that he inserted in her. I swore I smelled a stench when he did that and the doctor must've too because turned his face up.

"There is your baby." He pointed to the screen and you could see a small something in her stomach. I didn't know if I should be happy or not. I wanted kids but not by her. I know for a fact this was going to kill Maci.

"You are exactly sixteen weeks."

"How much longer does she have to get rid of it?" I ran my hand over my head as I asked.

"Khalid I'm not terminating this pregnancy." She said standing up to put her clothes on. I smelled that stench again and asked the doctor can he do a full exam on her because that smell was serious. She looked offended but I have zero fucks being I had been sleeping with her. He asked her if it was ok and I gave her a look daring her to say no. He put a facemask on and put some clamp in her. He used some q-tip looking thing and swiped inside her.

"All finished." He took his gloves off and kept the mask on.

"The results should be back in the next few days."

"Yo I need you to rush that shit. Whatever that smell is means she has something."

"If you're worried about it; it's probably in your best interest to be checked as well." He said hanging her a prescription for prenatal vitamins.

"Aren't you going to prescribe her something to clear that up?" I asked.

"I can't give her anything until we know for sure if she does. If I do it can affect the baby."

"I don't give a shit about that baby."

"KHALID." She yelled out.

"What? The first time I came in you I told you to get that abortion pill. You know I strapped up every day I slept with you after that. But you being the sneaky bitch that you are went ahead and trapped me. You need to make an appointment to terminate it."

"Sir if I can." He said and turned to face us. I nodded for him to speak.

"If she does terminate there's a chance she can never have kids again."

"I don't give two fucks about that. That's the problem with bitches these days thinking a baby is going to keep a man. Yea I messed up and slept with you unprotected but for you to take it upon yourself to make a decision like that on your own was selfish. That baby didn't ask to be here and you're now forcing it into a world where I won't even be a part of its life because it was made out of spite. This is exactly why I should've worked it out with Maci." I saw the doctor raise his eyebrows when I mentioned Maci's name.

"Khalid." Maribel was now crying.

"What?"

"Can't we just try and raise this baby together?"

"No. Call me a dead beat all you want. You know if this was something I really wanted my kid would want for nothing. Matter of fact I want a DNA test done and if that's my child I'm taking it. I'm not raising a baby with a bitch I can't stand. Yo I'm out because if I stay here any longer I can't say I won't keep my hands off you." I heard a knock at the door.

"Is everything ok I'm here doctor?"

"Yes. Can you show Mr. Khalid out?" This thirsty bitch licked her lips and showed me the way. As if my day couldn't get any worse.

"Khalid, what are you doing here?" Maci asked me. She stood there looking as beautiful as ever. I don't know what I was thinking messing up with her.

"I." I didn't even get a chance to finish my sentence before this stupid bitch opened her mouth.

"Hey Maci. Khalid did you tell her the good news?"

"What news?"

"Oh that we're expecting." The look on Maci's face was worse than when she found out I came in Maribel the night we broke up. Her eyes were getting glassy.

"Oh. Ok well I guess congratulations are in order."

"Maci."

"You don't have to explain Khalid. We're not together

and I knew it was going to happen."

"How you figure?" Maribel asked with her hands on her hips.

"It doesn't matter. You got what you wanted Maribel, and Khalid I guess you did too. I mean you wanted something I couldn't give you and now you have it. Don't send me a baby shower invitation because I can tell you right now I'm not coming. Enjoy your pregnancy. I heard it's a joyous thing." Maci ran out the doctors' office and I followed her with Maribel on my heels.

"Maci, I didn't know. She told me to meet her here and never said what it was about. I swear you're the only woman I want to have my kids. Baby, let's talk about this." She wiped the tears that continued to fall.

"There's nothing to discuss. Khalid I can't give you what she can, so be happy that you're about to be a dad." She sped off. I put my hands on top of my head and watched her. I don't ever think she'll be the same after this. How could I be so fucking stupid? I saw Maribel smirking.

"I don't know what you're doing that for. If I find out

you gave me something I'm going to kill you, pregnant or not." She removed that smirk right off her face.

"That's what I thought. Stay the fuck away from me." I hopped in my car and left her standing there looking stupid.

A few weeks later I pulled up to Gage and Meadows house and noticed Maci's car. I debated if I should go in or not but I didn't have to take long to make that decision because Gage opened the door for me shaking his head. He told me to come down to the basement to talk to him because the girls were dogging me out right now. I followed him but stopped when I overheard Maci saying she should move away so the baby wouldn't be thrown in her face.

"Let me talk to you for a minute." I snatched her up and took her in one of the guest rooms. I stood in front of the door and waited for her to come out the bathroom in there.

"Why aren't you out celebrating the good news?" She and I both knew she was being sarcastic.

"Cut it the fuck out Maci. You know damn well I'm not happy about this entire situation. Yes, I slipped up and got her pregnant but it doesn't change the fact that you're the only person I still want."

"Why do you want someone who can't give you the thing you want the most?"

"What do you think I want the most Maci since you seem to know it all?"

"Kids."

"Maci, of course I want kids; what man wouldn't. I'm so sorry about what happened to you in that hospital and how it messed up our chances of having kids. But Maci all you had to do was talk to your man. We could've gone to the doctor's together or even starting looking into adoption. Instead you went out with another man and discussed it all with him as if I didn't exist. How do you think that made me feel? I couldn't comfort you or even be there for you. Fuck. You put us in this situation trying to prove a point." She gave me the side eye.

"You may not have made me stick my dick in her but you damn sure pushed me to her."

"I'm sorry Khalid. I never took into consideration that you were affected or that I should've told you." She laid her head on my shoulder and I put my arm around her.

"Maci, believe me when I say I didn't know and I damn sure wouldn't have told you like that. I told her to terminate it and if she didn't and it turned out to be mine I was taking it from her. She's not fit to be anyone's mother and you and I both know that."

"Why did this have to happen to me?" She fell back on the bed and her shirt was up a little exposing her bare stomach. I leaned down and kissed it. She put her hand on my head. I unbuttoned her jeans and she lifted up so I could get them and her panties down. Her pussy smelled like that strawberry scent she showered with. I spread her legs and let my tongue slide up and down her slit.

"Make me cum Khalid." She moaned out. I parted her bottom lips again and wiped out all her juices. I wiped my face and moved up to kiss her. She wrapped her hands around my neck and invited my tongue in. I slid my shorts and boxers down and entered her and just laid there. My dick was thumping inside while her walls squeezed the hell out of my man.

"I missed you so much Khalid." She wiped the tears

that started to fall. I stroked her slow in the beginning and sped up once she got reacquainted with my size.

"I missed you too baby. I love you so much Maci and I'm sorry for sleeping with someone else when we had just broken up."

"Khalid, do you really love me." She asked when I had her climb on top.

"More than you can ever know." She went up and down, in circles driving me insane.

"Then let me go." She said as we both came together. She fell on my chest trying to catch her breath.

"Never and don't ever let me hear those words leave your mouth again." I lifted her face up and kissed her hungrily waking my man up again. She and I stayed in that room all night sexing each other down. When she was asleep I laid there watching her. This was the woman I was making my wife and we were going to get through everything together. All this breaking up because she was trying to prove a point was about to stop.

"I love you Khalid." I thought she was asleep but I

guess not.

"I love you too Maci and don't you ever forget it. We were made for each other and there's nothing keeping me from making you my wife." She turned over with tears in her eyes again.

"Stop crying. Why are you crying so much?"

"I'm pregnant."

Chapter 16

Maci

When I told Khalid I was pregnant I didn't expect him

to jump out the bed and get dressed leaving me there naked. I got up and went downstairs only to hear his car pulling off out the driveway. I wanted to tell him how what happened and that it was a miracle but he bounced before I could tell him anything. I know everyone must think I'm stupid for going out with the doctor and yes I was wrong. However, he actually gave me better news than I expected that day.

You see once I came home from the hospital and woke up I was made aware of the situation with them telling me I would have a hard time conceiving. I went to see a specialist once I heard about the miscarriage to find out how quick I could get pregnant again. You may wonder why a specialist well truth be told I am a woman who has been very cystic and every month before my period came I would always grow cyst on my ovaries but they would go away after my cycle. The doctors thought birth control would help but when they didn't I just stopped taking them altogether.

Anyway, the doctor told me everything I needed to do and started me with the process. I visited the fertility doctor, which was the guy someone sent him a picture of. I was having sex with Khalid two to three times a day hoping to get pregnant. Then every night injected myself with hormones. The shit hurt like hell but I wanted to have his babies. Unfortunately, his ex beat me to it. I blamed him and I had every right to. If he wanted to sleep with someone the least he could've done was strapped up. I know he claims to want me to be his wife but I'm not sure if I'm ok raising another woman's child. You can say I'm childish all you want but if I was pregnant by another man during our break up there's no way in hell he would be me ok with it.

I called and sent text messages for weeks to Khalid trying to get him to speak to me but every one of them went unanswered. I finally said screw him and went on about my life. I hadn't told anyone about the pregnancy besides him and my mom and I wanted to keep it that way. Today Melina was having a birthday party for Morgan because she was turning one. I knew Khalid would be there because that was his niece. We may not have been speaking but you can bet a bitch was going to be dressed to impress. I wore a pair of white jeans with cuts on the front of them. You know the kind all women wear these days. I had a black off the shoulder shirt that was baggy in the front and covered my belly perfectly. I put some strap up sandals on and let my hair flow down my back. I put light makeup on and sprayed the strawberry spray I got from Bath and Body works. I stepped out my car and Meadow met me at the door.

"Hey sis. Aren't you looking sexy?" She gave me a hug and we walked back into Bruno's house together. They were no longer an item in her eyes but they were still an item in his.

"Hey aunties baby." I picked up lil Javion and he started whining.

"That's weird. He goes to everyone." Meadow said taking him from me. They say when you're pregnant most babies can sense it and won't allow you to hold them. I didn't want anyone to know so I didn't say anything. I made me a plate and sat down next to Melina who was feeding Morgan, and my parents. There were a ton of Bruno's friends there with kids too. I lifted my head up to see who everyone was saying hi to and we locked eyes instantly. He looked damn good in his dark blue jeans, T-shirt and Balenciaga sneakers. He had on his necklace that was bright and what looked like a brand new Rolex. What caught my eye was the chick standing next to him?

"What the fuck? I know this nigga didn't bring that bitch here." I heard Meadow say causing Melina to look. She stood there smiling and allowing people to rub her stomach. I couldn't explain how mad I was but I kept my game face on. I wasn't about to let neither of them spoil my nieces' birthday. But I had a surprise for his ass. He wants to play games; well ok about to show him how to do it. I picked my phone up and sent a text to my friend. Luckily he was available to stop by.

"Yo you are disrespectful as fuck." Melina said to Khalid when he walked over to speak.

"It's ok Melina. He can sport his woman anywhere he wants. It's a free country. I'm not mad at all."

"That's not my woman she just."

"Nope."

"Maci." I heard Meadow call my name and I continued walking over to where Gage was. He gave me a hug and told me fuck him. If he doesn't want to do the right thing then leave him in the past because that's where he left me. I nodded and agreed with him. My phone chimed letting me know I had a text. My friend was telling me he was outside. I went to get him and had to take a second look. This man was just as fine as Khalid. I only saw him dressed that one night at the club with regular clothes but seeing him the second time made me want to jump his bones.

"You're looking sexy ma." Ma. I didn't even know he spoke street language. I guess you can't judge a book by its cover.

"Thank you for coming but I want to let you know he's here before you go back there. I don't want you to be blindsided."

"It's all good baby girl. We're just friends and I'm here to support you unless you need something else." He lifted my chin and kissed my lips. His tongue wrestled around with mine for a minute and I had to pull back before I took him home.

"Damn." I said out loud not realizing how it sounded.

"Was it good for you as it was for me?" He grabbed my hand and we stepped in the back together.

"Damn Maci. Who is that? He fine as hell." Meadow said making Gage pinch her in the arm. Melina just laughed because she had the same reaction when she first met him at the office with me. She had come there after Khalid found out I went on a date with him. I sent him a text ahead of time asking him to pretend that I wasn't pregnant yet because I wasn't ready to tell.

"Guys this is my friend Dr. Stanton. Dr. Stanton this is my mom, dad my sister Meadow and her boyfriend Gage and you know Melina." He shook everyone's hand and took a seat; pulling me down on his lap.

"Hey Dr. Stanton." Maribel came over to where we were.

"Hello Ms. Santos. A few more weeks huh."

"Yup. Khalid and I are so excited." She started rubbing her stomach. I know he felt me tense up because he wrapped his arms around my waist and kissed my shoulder.

"That's great. I guess I'll see you in the delivery room."

"Hey Maci is this your new friend. Khalid come meet your ex's new man." She yelled across the yard and he came over looking mad.

"Oh word Maci."

"Khalid not that I owe you an explanation but this is my friend Dr. Stanton. I'm sure you remember him being you saw him that day you claimed to have found out she was pregnant."

"Maci let me talk to you."

"For what?" Maribel said and it made me laugh on the inside.

"Yea for what?"

"Don't play with me Maci."

"Khalid I'm enjoying myself why don't you take your girlfriend and go do the same?"

"Yea Khalid come on. I want to tell one of the girls over there about how we decorated your son's room in the house." I saw him snatch her up quick as hell. She was being petty and he knew it but I was over the dumb shit with him. He didn't want to be with me; I couldn't force him. A few hours went by and Morgan opened her gifts and we sang Happy Birthday to her. Marcel who is the doctor got a page that one of his patients was in labor. I walked him out to the car.

159

"You ok." I put my head down and he lifted it back up.

"Yea I'll be alright. Thanks for coming to my rescue."

"Anything for you Maci. I know your heart is still with that man but if you ever find yourself looking for a real man and if I'm available I promise to treat you like you're supposed to be. A woman like you may have flaws like we all do but your heart is always in the right place." We started kissing again and this time I felt his dick pressing on my clit. As bad as I needed sex I could never allow him to penetrate me right now with another man's child in my stomach. He reached his hands in my jeans and I unbuttoned them so he could get better access to my swollen pearl that he woke up. The kissing was so intense that he had me cumming fast. He brought his fingers to his mouth and sucked all my juices off before letting me taste myself on his tongue.

"That pussy is just as sweet as I knew it would be."

"Well if you're a good boy maybe I'll come by tonight and let you see her and really get a taste."

"Don't play with me Maci."

"Yea don't play with him Maci." I heard his voice

160

behind me.

"Call me when you get finish so you can handle me." I whispered in his ear and he went to get in the car.

"Call me if you need me." He said when the window came down.

"She won't need you. I'm here." I saw Marcel laugh.

"Righhhhtttt." He pulled off and I started walking back inside. Khalid pulled my arm and swung me around to face him.

"What? What could you possibly want from me Khalid? Huh? I tell you I'm pregnant and before I can explain how it happened you got up and not only left but disappeared. Then I can't get in touch with you for weeks only to have you bring your fucking baby momma to my niece's birthday party. I know it's over and I haven't bothered you or Maribel so why can't you leave me alone? I told you to let me go the last time we slept together and you said no and I would still be your wife. You decided that's not what you wanted and as bad as it hurt I let you go. So please tell me what the fuck you want?" I was pissed, yelling and crying at the same time. He sipped his beer and just stared at me without saying a word.

"Goodbye Khalid." I said when I saw Maribel coming toward us.

"Maci." I walked away from him backwards so I could finish telling his ass off.

"No. Go finish decorating your son's room. You need to be prepared for when he gets here. If you didn't hear me before when I said it I'm going to say it again. I FUCKING HATE YOU KHALID." He ran past Maribel and snatched me up tossing me against the house. His face was in my neck.

"Take that shit back Maci."

"No. I hate you. I hate what you did to me. I hate that you got your ex pregnant. I hate that you left me when I told you I was carrying your child. The child we were supposed to be happy about. I hate that I'm going to have to raise it alone and I hate that another man will take your spot because you were being stupid. Leave me alone."

"I'm sorry Maci. I never."

"Stop it. Nothing you say means anything to me anymore. You say it then take it back with your actions. I'm giving you what you want. I'm letting you go." I wiped my eyes and looked up at him and he had his own tears coming down his face.

"Maci I can't live without you. Let's work this out."

"No. When I wanted to you left me hanging. I didn't know if anything happened to you because you wouldn't talk to me. You avoided me at all cost. How could you treat me like that? Me Khalid. I know I was mad because you got in my ass and was trying to teach me how to be grown and deal with grown up issues but you left me. YOU FUCKING LEFT ME NOT ONCE BUT TWICE. Let me go Khalid. Just let me go." I kissed his lips, wiped his tears and walked away.

"He's all yours. He finally let me go Maribel. Good luck with your family."

My heart was aching badly right now. I felt like I could die. I went in one of the rooms and cried myself to sleep.

Chapter 17

Maribel

I got a kick out of watching that bitch Maci get in her feelings about Khalid bringing me to the birthday party. I'm sure he didn't want me to go knowing she would be there but I eased my way into the car. I saw him at the mall picking the little girl up a few outfits and some sneakers. I went in the store with him and picked a few pair of Jordan's for my son I was carrying.

"What do you want Maribel?" I put the stuff on the counter. He sucked his teeth but paid for it anyway. Khalid was still refusing to do anything for the baby until he got a DNA test done. He must've been in a good mood because he paid for it and handed me the bag.

"Where are you going?"

"None of your fucking business." He hit the alarm on his truck and I got in the passenger side.

"Get out. I have somewhere to be." I didn't say anything and took his man out and gave him some pleasure to calm him down. Who knew he would start his ride up and take me with him? We ended up back at my house with him banging my back out. He got dressed after he washed up and headed out the door. I ran behind him and asked to come and he just said fuck it and to get in. The night didn't go well for him as I watched Maci tell him she didn't want him anymore after what he did to her but I thought I also heard her say she was pregnant. *Nah, she can't be. Not after what my cousin did. But she was at the gyn that day. Fuck.* If she's pregnant then he won't focus all his attention on the baby and me.

"Are you ok?" I asked him as he pulled into my driveway. It was like he was in a daze.

"KHALID." I yelled out making him snap out of whatever it was.

"Huh. What's up?"

"I said are you ok?"

"Don't ask me any questions. That petty shit you did is the reason why I don't take you anywhere?"

"What petty shit?"

"Telling everyone about your son's room being set up at my house."

"Who cares? No one needs to know we don't live together."

"Maci that is bullshit."

165

"I know the fuck you didn't just call me that bitch's name." I went to get out the car and caught a hand to my face. He backslapped the fuck out of me. I looked over at him and he was getting out the car. I tried to get out and run but didn't make it far.

"I told you before never to call her out her name and you do it anyway. Maribel I'm going to say this one more time. I don't know if that's my baby and until we know for sure stay the fuck away from me. Maci is where I want to be but some reason you keep messing shit up."

"I'm messing it up. Boy, you're the one who got mad at her and fucked me with no condom. You're the one who continued sleeping with me. You're the one who acts like he can't get it together so don't tell me I messed shit up. That was all you." I saw his facial expression change.

"You're right I messed up the one thing in my life that meant something to me. I shouldn't be blaming you when even though you're a petty bitch, its nobody's fault but my own. Goodbye Maribel."

"Khalid, why couldn't you love me the way you love

her?"

"Because she's different. She captured my heart from the moment I laid eyes on her. I got to genuinely know her before anything sexual happened. She is my one and only soul mate and I lost her over some dumb ego shit." His eyes were a little glassy. I couldn't believe that bitch broke him down the way she did. Her pussy must be made in platinum to get him like that. He didn't even cry when we broke up and we were together much longer. I watched him pull off and walked in my house to put the bags down.

"Is that my baby?" I jumped when I heard his voice.

"Who knows?"

"What you mean who knows?"

"You know what that means. I was sleeping with you faithfully without a condom and he slipped up once. Yes, I told him it was his because I'm not about to live like some bum bitch again. That nigga is going to take care of me whether he wants to or not."

"I thought I was on some grimy shit but I think you have me beat. What makes you think he's going to do anything for you when you're still living here?" I looked over my three-bedroom condo that Khalid brought me a few years ago and decided it was time for an upgrade. It was built a few years before I moved in here but I wanted something bigger now. Why should she get to live with him in that big house when they were together and I'm stuck in this condo? Khalid thought he was slick. I know he was secretly praying Maci came back to him that's why he never allowed me to his home but that's all going to change.

"What is your sneaky ass up to now?" He asked coming next to me and pulling my dress up.

"I see you got rid of that smell." I pushed his head away and put my dress down.

"Boy get out."

"I'm not going anywhere until I taste that pussy." I just grinned. I had no business sleeping with his crazy ass but his dick game was on point.

"My pussy is doing just fine." I thought about what he was talking about and got mad thinking about it. He and I had been messing around for a few months before Khalid supposedly got me pregnant. We never wore a condom and the day Khalid slipped up I prayed he got me pregnant and what do you know? Unfortunately, I was feeling sick before we slept together so I really have no idea who the daddy is. Anyway, Khalid never slipped up after that and used a condom every time but this nigga didn't. He fucked around and gave me Chlamydia and a yeast infection. I cursed his ass the fuck out. Luckily, Khalid didn't catch it after the first encounter and I was able to treat it without having to tell him.

"Did you take your medication?" Once I told him he took his ass down to the free clinic to be seen.

"Yup, now open up so I can eat." I did what he told me and laid there enjoying the way his tongue felt. Call me nasty all you want since I slept with Khalid earlier but a bitch stayed horny with this pregnancy. After we finished he ordered us some take out. We were lying in bed when someone started banging on my door.

"Go see who it is." He said smacking me on the ass. Nobody really came to my house. I was shocked as hell when I opened the door and my cousin was standing there with a gun in her hand pointing it at me.

"Girl, get your stupid ass in here."

"Where's my money?"

"I told you I would get it to you but you have to wait."

"I didn't know you were pregnant."

"Yes, and I need you to get back to work at the

hospital. Khalid asked for a DNA test so I need you to work

your magic and have it say he's the father."

"Hell no. You already got me in some shit and haven't

made good on the money. You think I'm about to put myself

out there again?"

"You're going to do what the fuck she says or your

brains are about to be all over this condo." My friend came out

with his gun pointed to her. I think she pissed herself because

her pants were now wet. I stood there with my arms folded and

a smirk on my face.

"Ok. Ok. Please don't kill me." Her hands were up and

she started backing up towards the door.

"I am calling the hospital later today to see if you're

there. Don't make me come looking for you?" I told her and

she ran out the house.

"You think she'll do it?" He asked and locked the door.

"Yea. My mom has her daughter and won't give her back until I say its ok."

"Hold up. Your mom is in on it?"

"Yea. She hates Maci's mom for some reason so anything to help me hurt his family she is down for it. She also knows how much my cousin loves her son. She won't jeopardize her son's life."

"How do you know? Shit, we see how you don't give a fuck about your other one."

"Oh she won't. You see the nigga she has the baby by has no idea he exist and she already knows if he finds out about him he will kill her and take him."

"What the hell y'all got going on?"

"My cousin was young, dumb and strung out on her baby daddy. They were together for a few years. She had just found out about the pregnancy and went by his house to tell him. Unfortunately, she walked in on him having sex with some chick. They ended up fighting, she left him and he moved on."

"Damn, did he look for her?"

"In the beginning he did but after a while he said fuck it. Now he's with the chick you fuck with and the crazy part is he did the same thing to her. It's like that nigga is a habitual cheater. The only difference between my cousin and that woman is he won't allow her to leave him. Shit, you know that first hand."

"Yea, he definitely is on some stalker type shit with her. I can't wait to taste that pussy. That nigga going crazy over her." I gave that nigga the side eye.

"What? You still fucking that nigga so don't look at me like that."

"Whatever. Don't get fucked up?"

"You wish you could beat me. Fix your face and give me some head. I'm tired and you know I like my dick sucked before I go to sleep."

"Yea alright." I gave him what he wanted but I couldn't sleep. I went into the living room to catch up on some shows and an idea popped up in my head. Bruno's birthday was coming up and word around town was he was having a huge

barbeque. What better place to let some secrets out than that. I

rubbed my hands together and laid down with a smile on my

face. I couldn't wait until the party in a few weeks. Shit was

going to hit the fan and I for one wanted front row seats.

Chapter 18

Melina

I'm glad Morgan's party was finally over. She received

so much stuff and her father seemed to be in his glory with us being there as a family last week. I'll admit that it did feel good being there with him but I know we were just living in the moment. Bruno may be a cheater but he is a damn good father and I will never take that away from him. I watched him basically stare at me the entire time and I enjoyed it. Making his ass sweat wasn't in my plans but that's what his ass gets. Thinking because he was a boss he could do what he wanted; well that nigga had another thing coming if he thought I was sitting around waiting.

"Mommy will see you tomorrow. I love you." I kissed my baby and walked out. She was staying with my parents for the night and I had a date. He wasn't taking me anywhere because I was still nervous about being seen out in the open so we were going to his house. He lived in some apartment complex a few towns over. I went home and cleaned myself up and drove to his house. He opened the door wearing just some sweats and some Nike slippers. Dude was sexy as hell and he wasn't even trying. He was tall, handsome and put me in the mind frame of someone I know but I didn't know who. His brown eyes were mesmerizing and his beard was what caught my eye with him.

"Don't you look nice?" He whisked me in the house and planted a wet kiss on my lips that ended up with me laid back in his bed with my pants down and his face in my pussy.

"Yes John Yes." I had my hand on his head as he dipped in and out with his tongue.

"Whoa buddy. I'm not with that shit." I backed up a little when he bit down a little too hard on my clit.

"I'm sorry ma. Let me make it better." He said and did exactly what he said. He had me moaning for a minute. He stood up and took his clothes off. His package made my mouth water.

"Ugh, condom boo." I can't believe he tried to go in raw.

"My bad. It taste so good I know the feeling is just as good."

"It is but you won't know that." I know how good my pussy is and the only one running in me unprotected is Bruno and since he's not here that aint happening. He pulled a brand new box from the drawer and opened it up along with the wrapper. If he didn't have any I sure did.

"Damn baby. This pussy tight and good as hell." He stroked me slow. His dick was definitely good. I started fucking him from underneath and he was losing his mind. I told him to let me get on top and this nigga started yelling out my name.

"Shit Melina, this pussy is so fucking good. Ahhh I'm about to cum. Melina, Melina oh shit Melina." He yelled out and filled the condom up with his sperm. He pulled my face to his and started kissing me aggressively and I felt his dick getting hard again. We had sex two more times and each time I checked those condoms to make sure they didn't break. If a nigga tried to get up in me raw the first time there's no telling how many he's done that with.

"You're not staying the night?" He asked standing behind me while I put my clothes on.

"No. You're not my man and I'm not comfortable staying somewhere you have a chick living at."

"What are you talking about?" I waved my hand at all

the woman stuff scattered around the house. I opened the closet door and sure enough there was women's clothing.

"That's my sister's stuff."

"Righhhhtttt." I said going to the door.

"Call me tomorrow then." He stood in the doorway and watched me until I pulled off. I called Maci up to tell her and she was just as excited as I was. I'm going to call you back when I get in the house. I opened the door and Bruno and Khalid were sitting in my living room playing some game. This was all the time with Bruno but I was shocked to see Khalid. I hope he wasn't planning to see Maci because she moved out a few weeks ago.

"How was the dick?" Bruno asked when I got out the shower.

"It was pretty good. How was the pussy you fell into after the party?" He thought I didn't see him talking to some chick that came. I wasn't mad though because we weren't together. He threw me against the wall and sniffed me.

"Nigga, I washed him off and yes I used a condom. I sure hope you did."

"Word Melina. It's like that."

"You made it that way. You got some nerve. Walking around slinging dick form chick to chick and you think I'm supposed to sit around and listen to all the stories?"

"What stories?"

"Bruno, everyone knows we used to be together. Every chance they get I hear a chick rubbing it in my face on how she had you and how you put it down in the bedroom. You think I want to hear that shit? At least I'm being discreet with my mine. No nigga can ever tell you anything about me." I felt the tears falling and was mad because I was done crying over him; at least I thought I was.

"Melina, I'm."

"I know sorry right. I'm over it Bruno." I waved him out the way and put my pajamas on. I sat down on the edge of the bed and listened to him and Khalid go back and forth over the game. I called Maci up but she told me her doctor friend was over. I know for a fact she wasn't over Khalid and the doctor knew too. I hung up and laid down on the bed. A few minutes later I felt Bruno behind me pulling my body closer to his.

"I love you with everything in me Melina and I swear I haven't slept with any woman since the day you saw me in the store." I turned over and he wiped my tears with his fingers. I still loved him but I know that his cheating was a problem.

"I love you too Bruno but I don't want to be that woman who takes you back and then you continue to do it over and over. Bruno I want to spend the rest of my life with you but right now you can't give me stability, honesty or all of you."

"Baby, I can give you all of that. I know you're scared but I promise that if you take me back this last time I won't even look in another woman's direction. You can go anywhere I go. Melina, I don't want to have to kill you." I sat up on my elbows and stared at him. The look in his eyes showed me he wasn't playing.

"Bruno I'm telling you right now if I find out you cheated again you won't have to kill me because I will kill you where you stand."

"You're definitely my gangster bitch." He kissed on my

neck.

"And don't think I'm taking you back because I'm scared of you because that's the not the case. I really want us to be a family for Morgan."

"I do too."

"Mmmmm that kiss is about to start something we can't finish right now." He looked at me.

"End that shit right now." He reached over and passed me my cell and had me dial John's number.

"Hey baby. You miss me already."

"Nah, nigga she doesn't miss you."

"Who the fuck is this?"

"Her man. Whatever y'all had ends now."

"That's too bad because that pussy is the best I ever had." I heard him say and Bruno's face was tight.

"Listen here partner. You damn right it is and the minute I find you your ass will be taking a dirt nap. No nigga that tasted my wife's pussy will live to tell it."

"Nigga aint nobody scared of you. You're worried about her when you should be worried about her other two sisters that I'm going to fuck soon enough."

"What you just say?" John disconnected the call.

"Who the fuck is that nigga?" He had me by the top of my pajama shirt.

"Bruno, I met him when we first broke up. He's from a few towns over."

"Give me the fucking address now." I gave him the address and listened to him tell Gage that he needed to keep an eye on Meadow. Khalid left not too long ago and wasn't answering his phone so Bruno left him a message telling him to get back to him. I sat against the bed crying with my knees to my chest. I just slept with a man who planned on going after my sisters what the hell was going on?

Chapter 19

Gage

Bruno called me in the middle of the night informing me of some nigga that Melina was messing with just threatened my girl and her sister. No one met the dude John but that wasn't going to be a problem because today we were going by his house. The address was out of town but the moment we pulled up I felt something wasn't right. We got out and Khalid asked me if I was ok. I nodded my head and pulled my phone out to call and check on Meadow. She went back to work for the first time since she had my son. I wasn't feeling it being though my brother was missing but she assured me if anything happened she would call.

"I haven't been gone that long and yes baby I'm safe." She answered before I was able to say hello. I smiled because she was always trying to boss up.

"I'm just checking. Is security at their post?" I asked waiting for someone to answer the door.

"Yes baby. Gage are you ok? Thank you and I will get back to you in a few." I could hear her talking to someone in the background.

"I'm good now that I know you're safe. I love you and I'll be by to take you out for lunch."

"Oh baby I have a lot of work to catch up on. Can you

bring it to me and we have lunch in my office. Pleaseeeee?"
She whined and made me laugh.

"Yea. Text me what you want and I'll make sure you get it."

"Hmmm I may not want food. Listening to how sexy your voice is I may want something else."

"Meadow, you're going to fuck around and I'm going to have you pregnant again."

"Who says I don't want that?"

"WHAT THE FUCK?"

"Gage what's wrong?"

"Meadow let me call you back." I didn't wait for her to answer. I stepped in front of Bruno and Khalid who were walking out shaking their heads. There were pictures of Meadow dressed in pajamas, some had her naked and in certain sexual positions with me in our bedroom. There was some of her in the kitchen and other parts of the house but the main one that stood out was the one of her and I in the office the day we watched the video of my mom trying to set me up.

"How the fuck? This motherfucker has cameras in my

house." I started ripping the photos off the wall and tearing the room up. I was so mad I lit a match and set the entire apartment on fire. I'll be damned if another man will see my wife. I found a laptop on the way out and picked it up to take to our computer guy. I called up the guy who put our security cameras in and had him meet me at my house. I made sure to take him out back where there were no cameras just in case he was watching.

"Tell me right now how the fuck this happened?" I had the dude bloody as hell in the chair.

"I don't know. I set up the cameras like your friend asked me then some guy came when he left and told me to make sure I emailed him all the information and to set him up an account."

"What kind of account?"

"The account that allows you to see what's going on in your home when you're not there. I swear I didn't know who he was. I assumed he was someone you know because y'all looked alike." When he said that I froze. Khalid and Bruno looked at me. *Nah, my brother isn't that smart to pull something off like this. Is he? How the hell did he know when*

the people would be at my house? And is he the one that

Melina slept with? No I don't and won't believe that shit. I

untied the guy and helped him up. I called our personal doctor

up and had him fix dude up. I went to my safe and handed him

two hundred thousand dollars in cash and told him to keep his

mouth shut. If I ever heard of him mentioning what I did his

two kids will be dead before he could blink.

"You think it's your brother?" Khalid asked on the way

to my moms' house. If anyone knew where he was it would be

her. That is her pride and joy. We pulled up just as some car

was speeding out. The guys looked at me but we just shrugged

our shoulders.

"Get that motherfucker." I heard my grandmother

yelling and running out the door in her robe. We all looked at

her like she was crazy.

"What's going on?"

"Your fucking brother tried to rape me and your stupid

ass mother tried to act like she didn't know what was going

on."

"Calm down grandma and tell me what happened." She lit a cigarette and her hands were shaking like crazy.

"Your brother came over and I started yelling at him for what he did to Meadow?" She had become really close with my girl since the night she beat my mom's up. She called Meadow her daughter from another mother.

"This nigga told me he and Meadow had some secret affair but when I called him out on it he got mad and went to your mom's room. I got in the shower and I heard someone open the door. I figured it was your mom using the bathroom or something until that crazy motherfucker got in the shower with me and started trying to put his dick in me. I beat the shit out of his ass. He ran out the bathroom and out the house. I went to see what your mother was doing and she was in her room watching television without a care in the world. Where they do that at?" My grandmother may be in her early fifties but she was still hood.

"She's exaggerating. Jesse didn't know she was in the shower." My mom said in a calm voice.

"He didn't know I was in the shower. You stupid bitch

who the fuck started the water? He sure as hell didn't. Let me get the fuck out of here before I kill her my damn self."

"I don't understand how the two of you can go against your own blood. Jesse has done nothing to either of you and yet you treat him like shit. I want you out of my house and I never want to see you again." My grandmother nodded her head and looked at me.

"Grandma you know you got a place to stay with me."

"Thank you but I don't want to put you out."

"Meadow loves you and so does my son. She will be more than happy for you to stay with us." I looked down at my phone while she got her things and noticed I had twelve missed calls from Meadow. My heart was racing as I waited for her to pick up.

"Baby, get to Melina's house now." She yelled in the phone and everyone heard her. Bruno looked up at me and took off out the house. We were right behind him in the car. He jumped out the car before I was able to stop. There were two police cars outside her crib. Maci was getting out the car and for a minute she looked pregnant. We walked up and overheard

Melina telling the officer that some guy she used to mess with came to her house and tried to attack her. He kicked her door in when she wouldn't let him in and they started fighting. You could see her clothes were ripped and her eye was a little black. Now we had the dude she used to mess with and my brother on the hit list.

"You good baby." I heard Bruno ask her. She was sitting on his lap crying.

"Bruno, how did he find out where I stayed? He's never been here."

"I don't know but you can guarantee I'm going to find his ass and its lights out. Get you and my daughter shit; you're not staying here anymore." She got up and Maci helped her pack a few things. After they left I called Meadow to let her know her sister was good and that I was on my way to get her. She was going to work from home until we had things under control. I couldn't have her out there blind.

"How you been Maci?" I asked her as she was putting more things in the bag for Morgan. We walked in the living room.

"I'm good Gage. Just been a little tired lately that's all." She glanced over at Khalid who was on the couch watching her every move.

"You know he loves you right?"

"I know. But right now, us being apart is probably the best thing for us."

"I'm just going to say this and then I'm out of it." She nodded her head and stood against the wall listening.

"Khalid has never loved a woman the way he loves you. I know that because we've been boys all my life. He told me everything that happened and he's fucked up about this baby with Maribel. You know he found out when she was four months and tried to get her to terminate it?" She covered her mouth.

"Maci, he doesn't want any woman to have his kids but you and if you can't then he's willing to adopt or not have any at all. I'm not saying how he handled the situation was right but the way his feelings are set up he's just as scared as you are. He may not tell you but it's the truth. When you told him you were pregnant he thought you were lying to keep him.

When he left he came straight to my house. The reason he ignored you was because he never thought you would try to trap him."

"But I didn't."

"Look at it from his point of view. You told him you couldn't have kids, you find out about Maribel, then you say you're pregnant. Not only that you went out on a date with another man and told him all your business. He was really fucked up and by the looks of it he had every right to believe you trapped him because you don't look pregnant to me and your sister would've told me."

"What do I need to trap him for? I have my own money, my own car, I go to school and if I need help my family is there. I don't need him for anything."

"Ah but you do." She gave me the side eye.

"You need him to love and comfort you. You need him to make you feel like you're the only woman in the world. You don't want him with another chick. Trapping a nigga doesn't always mean with his money or his baby. In his case you tried to trap his heart. Before you ask let me fill you in on what I mean. Trapping his heart means you will have him to any and everything for you; yet you refuse to do the same for him and because you have his heart he won't let you go and allow you to treat him like shit and that's not right."

"I would ever expect him to allow me to walk all over him."

"You may not see it Maci but you already have." I kissed her cheek and walked out. I thought he would stay and comfort her but his ass was right behind me. I dropped him off and went to pick my girl up.

"That girl still loves you."

"I know."

"What are you going to do?"

"Nothing man. She said some things to me that were pretty fucked up. I just don't think I can sit back and watch her be with another nigga when she's pregnant with my kid." I stopped short and looked over at him.

"She's really pregnant?"

"That's what she told me. I don't thinks she has a reason to lie and I was staring at her stomach. She did get thick and her hips spread."

"But I thought?"

"I did too. I guess they had it wrong."

"What are you going to do about Maribel?"

"I don't know. To be honest I don't think it's my baby. She's due in two weeks and all I can do is wait and go from there. I can't ask Maci to raise a kid with me that I conceived with someone else because I was mad. That would be expecting too much. That's why after Morgan's party and she said all those things I let her be. If it's meant for us to be back together it has to be because she wants to." I nodded my head because I understood loud and clear what he was saying.

"Keep your head up." We dapped each other up and he walked in his house. I went to get my girl and make sure she was good. Plus, my grandmother was still at Melina's crib with Maci waiting for me to come back and get her. This has been a long stressful day. All I want to do is get my girl, my son and go the fuck home.

"Hey baby." Meadow said and kissed me when she got in the car.

"Hey."

"You looked stressed."

"I am."

"Hmmm let mami handle it for you." She bent down and allowed me to release in her mouth. I must say that was all it took for me to feel better. I had to change seats with her. That nut drained the hell out of me.

"I love you Meadow."

"I love you too. Let's go home so I can ride my dick." She laughed and continued driving.

"Don't say shit to me when you get pregnant again." I told her and put my seat back to rest my eyes. I loved everything about my life and I was making sure my brother wasn't going to destroy it.

Chapter 20

Bruno

It's been pretty quiet since that fuck nigga attacked my girl. We still couldn't find Jesse's punk ass but you can bet his time was surely limited. Melina and my daughter were now living with me again and a nigga was happy as hell. She made me call all my bitches up and cancel them. It was funny because the only one who gave her a hard time was Shana. She had my son but I had custody of him and she was mad as hell. Yes, money made the world go round. I didn't want to take Shana from her but after she had my son Melina was already done with me.

I went by Shana's house and the bitch was drunk and high. My son was only two weeks old and screaming at the top of his lungs. I picked him up, changed him and gave him a bottle. All of this while she was passed the fuck out. Of course a nigga took a picture of the house and a video of me trying to wake her stupid ass up. She was so gone that she didn't call me until the next day panicking about someone kidnapping my son. I laughed at her dumb ass and told her I had him. Yup, the judge got a whiff of the photos and videos and gave me full custody right away. Ever since then she's been trying to get in my good graces by offering me sex. She may have been good in bed but she was a horrible mother and I was going to make it

194

right with Melina.

"Baby, bring me Junior's bottle." Melina yelled down the steps to me. I had Morgan asleep on my shoulder and was on my way to putting her in the room. My kids were my world and so was Melina. I didn't think you could love anyone more than yourself until the three of them came along. We were trying to get them settled before we left out to go to the barbeque I was throwing for myself. My parents were coming over to get the kids and Melina being the mommy she is had to make sure they were changed and fed first. I didn't think she would be ok with helping me raise him but I was wrong. She catered to him as if he were her own.

"Melina, you're not even dressed yet." I almost yelled out. I hated when we had somewhere to be because she always took forever getting ready.

"I already took a shower but he woke up and you know I can't leave my son crying like that." I grinned when she said that. She wasn't trying to be his mom but she also wasn't going to ignore the fact that she may have to be if Shana didn't get it together. I planned on giving him back to her but right now she was showing me that's not what she wanted. I'll be damned if I sent him back to that hellhole.

"Bruno, stop staring at me like a creep." She hated when I did that. After she fed and burped him I took him from her so she could get dressed. It's been a few months since I've seen her body and my mouth was watering when she took the robe off exposing her naked underneath. She stood in front of the dresser taking her underclothes out.

"What you want to taste this?" She turned around grinning.

"You know I do." This would be our first time in a while being intimate. I've been ready but she wanted to wait at least two weeks because she slept with that fuck nigga and said it was a waiting period to sleep with another person. No idea where she got that from but whatever. The two weeks past and here I was head first in her pussy while she screamed and moaned.

"Get up Melina. I want to fuck the shit out of you and get you pregnant again." She scooted back on the bed and put her index finger in her mouth making this sexy ass face. I don't think my dick could get any harder than it was.

"You are one sexy motherfucker." I told her and entered her slowly. She pushed my chest up a little and told me to go slow. The sounds of her pussy drove me crazy. I stroked her slow over and over.

"I missed you Bruno." She said and wrapped her arms around my neck and kissed me like it was her last time.

"I missed you too baby. I won't mess up again. I promise." She and I went on for about an hour. I came so hard I had to lie there for a few minutes to catch my breath.

"You know you're pregnant now."

"Are you ok with that?" She asked and got back in the shower. I went in there with her and swung her to face me.

"What you mean by that?"

"Because it's not in your OCD plan."

"Melina, I know I hurt you and I also know my OCD is crazy. I've been seeing someone for it and before you ask it's a male. He's been helping me cope with it. I know you may not be ready to get married but I want you to have my kids until we do. I love the fuck out of you girl." She grinned and hopped in my arms; grinding on my dick.

"Hell no. We are not about to fuck again."

"Why not?"

"Melina we are already a half hour late."

"Fine. I'm just going to talk to my friend real quick."
She said and took me in her mouth and had me moaning out
like a bitch. We finally got dressed and I must say my girl was
bad. She was rocking a pair of those high shorts but her ass
wasn't hanging out. Her shirt was a classy tank top type and
her sandals had to be wrapped up around her leg. I don't know
what you call it. Her hair was curly and pushed up in a bun and
her makeup was light but perfect. My girl was definitely the
definition of a bad bitch.

"I'm ready."

"Shit. I don't know if I want to leave." I grabbed my
man.

"I got you later. You know that." She stepped in front
of me and went downstairs to give the kids who were now
awake and sitting in the living room with my parents a kiss.

The park was packed with niggas and bitches

everywhere. Luckily I had a few parking spots blocked off for my boys and me. I helped her out the car and from the side I swore I saw my ex Theresa. She and I used to be hot and heavy until she walked in on me fucking someone else. I wasn't even mad when she told me she was leaving town because I broke her heart. I was young and she was feeling me way more than I was with her. I guess that's what happens when you sleep with a virgin.

"Where the fuck is my son?" We heard Shana behind us. When Melina turned around you could see how tight her face got. She was dripping with jealousy, hate and envy all at once.

"He's at home being well taken care of." Melina said and stood in front of me. I put my hands around her waist and kissed her neck. We both knew it was pissing her off not only seeing me happy but seeing me with the same woman that she thought I left alone. I always told her and any other chick I fucked around with no one and I mean no one will ever come before Melina or my kids.

"Bitch was I talking to you."

"Baby, I see Maci and Meadow. Handle this and come see me when you're done." Melina said sticking her tongue in my mouth. I squeezed her ass and made sure she could feel how hard she got me.

"I love you."

"I love you too baby." I told her and watched her walk off.

"If you ever disrespect my girl like that again I'll kill you." I told her as I held her up in the air by her throat. Gage had to come over and pry my hands off her. Her body hit the ground so hard I saw blood coming from her nose. I hated when a bitch tested me and this one did it quite often. I bet she won't do it again. An hour went by and I had Melina by my side while we mingled with the rest of the people.

"Baby, I'll be back." Melina whispered in my ear. I got up from the card table and pulled her to the side.

"Where you going?" I wasn't taking any chances of letting her out of my sight. We were in a public place and there was no telling if that nigga was lurking.

"I'm just going to the bathroom. Maci is coming with

me."

"Yo, are you pregnant?" I looked at Maci and it looked like all the color drained from her face. I turned around and Khalid was walking in with Maribel. I couldn't understand why he kept bringing this bitch with him. He couldn't stand her but she was always around.

"No she's not pregnant silly. She would've told me by now."

"It sure looks like it and you've gone to the bathroom with her at least six times since we got here."

"Don't be clocking my bathroom runs Bruno." She yelled at me and started walking away. Khalid went running after her and Maribel stood there with her big ass stomach looking like the dumb bitch she was.

"Hey Bruno."

"What the fuck you want?"

"Oh nothing. I just wanted to let you know my cousin was in town."

"And."

"And she wanted to see you. I'm surprised she hasn't

popped up yet." I knew I saw my ex lurking.

"Listen Maribel, I don't know what type of shit you on, but I can tell you right now pregnant or not I will beat your ass out here."

"You would hit a pregnant woman?"

"Bitch, that's not my boy's baby. The sooner you have it the quicker he can get the test and you'll be out of his life."

"Whatever. If I were you I would be looking out for my cousin. She has some extravagant news to tell you. I can't wait to see your face."

"Bitch beat it." I looked around the park to see if I saw Theresa but she was gone like the wind. I sat back down and looked in the direction Melina was. I saw her arguing with some dude and took my strap out. That caused everyone at the table to do the same.

Chapter 21

Maci

"What do you want Khalid?" I stood there with my arms folded looking at Melina go in the bathroom.

"I want to talk to you."

"Fine. Let me use the bathroom and then we can talk." I went in one of the stalls and handled my business. I was almost four months and the baby had me using the bathroom every twenty minutes it seemed like. I washed my hands and noticed Melina staring a hole in my face. Meadow walked in and asked what was going on.

"I think this bitch is pregnant." Meadow lifted my shirt up before I could stop her.

"You fucking bitch. Why didn't you tell anyone? Is Khalid the father?"

"Where is the respect? Why you pulling my clothes up like that?"

"Hell no. We're asking the questions. Why didn't you tell anyone?"

"Yes, I am pregnant and the only people who know are mommy and my baby's daddy. I was scared to tell anyone. I didn't want to lose it and with everything going on it was a chance it could happen."

"Girl. I can't believe we are about to aunties." Meadow

said rubbing my stomach. After a few minutes we went outside and Khalid was still standing there. Meadow and Melina walked over to the table where Gage was.

"I see you told them." He was sitting on a chair and pulled me down on his lap.

"You heard them huh?"

"Yea." He rubbed my stomach and at that very moment everything seemed so right between us.

"I miss you Maci."

"I miss you too. Why did you leave me Khalid?" I laid my head on his shoulder.

"When you told me you were pregnant I was happy and sad at the same time. You were messing with that guy and I wasn't sure if it was mine. Then you told me you couldn't have kids."

"I know but." He didn't let me finish.

"Maci, I will always take care of my kids you know that but I would never ask you to take care of a kid I made because I was mad at you. I messed up and now I have to face my consequences."

"Is that your baby?"

"I don't know. I won't until she has it and I get it tested. Maci, I want you to believe me when I say you're the only woman I ever want to birth my kids but I messed up."

"It's ok Khalid. All you can do is take care of it and pray for the best because you can believe she's about to try and get everything out of you."

"Nah. I told her if that's my kid I'm taking it. There's no way I'm allowing her to raise my kid and she doesn't even have the other one."

"Khalid."

"No Maci. She's not a good mother, which is why I never wanted a kid by her when we were together. It doesn't matter if you're with me or not she and I will never be together." He pulled my head down to his and divided my lips so his tongue could make an entrance.

"Mmmmm I miss your tongue." He said. I pulled him back to me and kissed him again. We were so into it we didn't stop until we heard someone clearing their throat.

"What the fuck you want?"

"Khalid, my water broke." He glanced down at her and you could see liquid dripping down her legs from the shorts she had on. I thought he would be in a rush but he took his time getting up.

"Can I call you later?" I shook my head yes and asked him for his phone. I told him I had to put my new number in it.

"I love you Maci."

"I love you too. Congratulations." He walked back to me.

"Don't do that? Maci, I'm not happy about this anymore than you are but I have to at least find out. You own my heart don't forget that." He pecked my lips and walked her to the car. I watched them pull off. I turned around looking for Melina when I noticed she was arguing with some dude on the side of the bathroom. I went over there at the same time I noticed Bruno running over with some guys. Gage must've noticed because he took Meadow off his lap and walked over there.

"Now that the gangs all here let me get started." He snatched Melina by the arm and put a gun to her head. Bruno and everyone else had theirs pointing at him.

"Jesse."

"Jesse. As in your brother Jesse?" Melina asked Gage. When he nodded his head she started vomiting.

"That's right Melina you fucked the man that almost slept with your sister and kidnapped her." Meadow and I covered our mouths. Bruno looked at Melina and you could tell he was mad.

"Bruno, I didn't know. He told me his name was John."

"What do you want Jesse?" Gage asked him.

"Your girl." Meadow started walking towards him.

"What the fuck you're doing Meadow?"

"Gage, I can't allow him to kill my sister. If he wants me then just let me go."

"FUCK NO. IS YOU CRAZY?"

"Gage, he's going to kill Melina. Please just let me go."

"Meadow, I know you're scared but you see that nigga Bruno right there. He is not about to allow him to take your sister from him. Don't think for one minute that my brothers not about to die."

"But."

"No buts. Look at me Meadow." He shook her but her eyes were still on Jesse who was smiling like a Cheshire cat and licking his lips.

"Gage."

"Meadow go get in the car with Maci." He nodded for some dude to come get us and in seconds a gun went off and Melina's body hit the ground.

"No, no, no." I ran over to her and Bruno was cradling her in his lap. The blood was gushing out her back.

"Melina, it's going to be ok baby. I swear you're going to make it. Please don't leave me baby." Bruno was crying while gunfire was going on behind me. Meadow passed out and hit the ground. Her head was bleeding and Gage was holding her.

The sirens were getting louder and louder as I watched one of my sisters' bleed out and the other one most likely had a concussion. The EMT's had to pry Melina out of Bruno's lap. His clothes were full of blood.

"Boss, he's gone." One of Bruno's men said to him.

"What the fuck you mean he's gone?"

"Some chick was waiting for him in a truck. I shot him a few times so he will have to get to a hospital." We stayed there for a few minutes after the ambulance left. Gage rode with Meadow and I tried to call Khalid but he didn't answer. I know she was in labor but fuck that his brothers needed him, I needed him.

"Bruno lets go." I said and he turned around to me.

"We have to go to the hospital to check on Melina and Meadow." I grabbed his shirt and he followed me to my car. We were all sitting in the emergency room when some chick came in dressed in scrubs and stared at Bruno. I tapped his leg and asked him who she was.

"Theresa. What the fuck are you doing here?" *Theresa.* That was the nurses' name that cared for me when I was in the hospital.

"Bruno. What are you doing here?" She asked like she was scared. When our eyes connected I jumped up and tried to kill that bitch. I hit her with punch after punch. Bruno finally broke us up and asked me what was going on. When I told him he wanted to beat her ass himself.

"I'm sorry. I had to do it or she was going to have that guy kill my son."

"So you make sure I can never have kids. You have a fucking kid but you tried to destroy my chances."

"I'm sorry please understand."

"Understand. Understand bitch I should kill you right now." I stood over her with Bruno's gun.

"Why did you do it?" She started telling us that her cousin had her son kidnapped and was supposed to pay her to kill me slowly so she could get to Khalid. The chick never paid her the money and she still couldn't get her son back.

"Yo, get her the fuck out of here and take her to the warehouse."

"Wait. Who the fuck is your cousin?"

"Maribel." When she said it, it was as if someone knocked the wind out of me. I felt myself hyperventilating. I took off and pressed the elevator. I couldn't get to labor and delivery fast enough. I asked them what room she was in because I was her sister that just came back in town. They pointed me in her direction. I opened the door and Khalid was helping her get out the bed. I started beating the brakes off that bitch.

"Maci, what are you doing? She's pregnant."

"Fuck that bitch and her baby." I pointed the gun at her stomach. The bitch had the nerve to be crying.

"What's going on?" He took the gun from me and sat it on the bed.

"If you turned answered your phone you would've known." I saw him feel around for it while he held me in the corner.

"I must've left it in the car. What's going on and why does it look like blood is on your clothes?"

"Khalid, I just came by to tell you the reason I can't have any more kids is because." That was the last thing I said before I felt the burning sensation in my arm and then my side. My body hit the floor and I heard Khalid's voice but had no idea what he was saying.

Chapter 22

Khalid

I turned around and Maribel was standing there holding

the gun with a smirk on her face. I threw her ass against the wall and snatched the gun out of her hand. Maci was on the

floor bleeding out and there was nothing I could do but yell out

for a doctor. I hid the gun in my back because it probably had

bodies on it. The nurses and doctors came rushing in and took

Maci out, then checked on Maribel. Her face was fucked up

and believe it or not she got back in the bed as if nothing

happened. I saw blood coming down her leg and all of a

sudden she was in pain. I wanted to walk out but I also didn't

want to miss the birth just in case it was my son.

"Ms. Santos it's time to push." She grabbed my hand

and I should've snatched it back but I didn't. I started telling

her to push with the doctors. An hour later she pushed a baby

boy out. He didn't have a look to him and before I could leave

out the room the nurse placed him in my hands. He was tiny

and hadn't opened his eyes yet. This was the moment I was

supposed to be experiencing with Maci; yet I was here with my

ex bonding with a baby that may not be mine.

"Where are you going?" Maribel asked me when I put

the baby back in the hospital crib.

"To check on Maci. If you killed her or my baby I'm

doing the same in return."

"Your baby."

"Yes, she is pregnant."

"But I thought."

"You thought what?" I waited to see if she would answer but she didn't.

"You're just going to leave your son to check on that bitch."

"We both know that may not be my kid. And I've told you about calling her a bitch." I walked over and pressed down on her stomach really hard until she screamed out. I may not hit a woman but Maribel pushed all my buttons and I was damn sure going to make her feel some sort of pain. I went to the surgery floor and they told me she was still in surgery and that they were trying to save the baby. The nurse directed me to a waiting area where I saw Bruno who was covered in blood; Gage had some blood on him but not as much, and the girls' parents.

"Yo, what happened when I left?" They started telling me when I saw someone walking towards us with a gun.

"Which one of you niggas is Bruno?" he had his gun pointed at Bruno and my gun along with a few others was pointed at him.

"Who wants to know?"

"The motherfucker that's been raising your son."

"Nigga you haven't been raising my son because he lives with me." Bruno said standing up.

"Nah, the one with Theresa." After he said that he started shooting and the hospital was like a war zone. I guess he came with a few people of his own. Thank goodness the girl's parents' had got up when he first stepped in. You could hear cop cars in the distance. I looked down and Bruno was bleeding from his chest. The other dude was barely hanging on.

"Somebody better get in here and make sure my brother lives or I'm killing every one of you." I yelled out. Doctors came running and that's when I noticed Rylee and Jesse standing by the door smiling. I went to run after them but by the time I got to the door they were gone. I had to find a way to make all this go away. There were cameras all through this hospital. I put a call in to the one nigga I knew could make all this go away with one phone call.

"Miguel, this is Khalid. I need your help."

TO BE CONTINUED...

CPSIA information can be obtained
at www.ICGtesting.com
Printed in the USA
LVHW011617090820
662758LV00003B/392